STAGECOACH STATION 48:

BUFFALO
STATION

Buffalo Station, Wyoming Territory 1886

BUFFALO

Big Horn Mts.

Powder River

MONTANA

ID.

WYOMING

AREA SHOWN
IN MAIN MAP

N. Platte R.

CHEYENNE
CITY

UTAH

COLORADO

THERESA

North

Platte

Rattlesnake
Hills

SODA LAKE

Sweetwater River

Laramie Mountains

FT. LARAMIE

River

R O C K Y

M O U N T A I N S

MEDICINE
BOW

0 5 10   20 30   40
MILES

CHEYENNE CITY

© BOOK CREATIONS INC. 1989

R. TOELKE '89

Prologue

It was an early afternoon in the middle of May 1886, and Theresa, Wyoming, was a busy little town. Wagons were parked in front of the business establishments lining both sides of the one long street, while the board sidewalks were crowded with men and women looking in shop windows or hurrying to and fro, attending to whatever it was that had drawn them into town that day.

Five men rode in from the south end of town onto that commercial scene, and a few of the passersby glanced at the leader, a medium-sized man with a cadaverous face, a full, sweeping mustache, and dark, piercing eyes. Zeke Slade and his fellow riders surveyed the town carefully, studying the rooflines of the false-fronted buildings, looking into the open doorways, and peering down the alleyways. The outlaws, who were wanted all over Wyoming Territory, entered any town the same careful way, knowing that at any given time they might well ride into an ambush of lawmen, vigilantes, or just good citizens.

"What the hell? Is this Saturday?" Luther Murdock asked, scratching his dark stubbly beard.

"How am I supposed to know?" Slade replied, pulling the brim of his Stetson down tighter on his head. "I don't keep no damn calendar."

"Seems to me like there's just too many people here," Murdock observed.

"Maybe that's to the good. The more people in the street, the easier it'll be for us to get away," Slade responded.

"There! There's the bank right down there on the corner, just like I said," one of the other men, Jim Silverthorn, pointed out. He nodded so vigorously that his stovepipe hat almost fell off his head.

"How much money you reckon's in it, Slade?" Slim Hawkins asked, his cold blue eyes lighting up with greed.

"I don't know. Maybe a couple of thousand dollars. Maybe more. It don't make no difference. A bank's a bank, and money's money."

"How are we goin' to do this? We just goin' to ride right in and hit it, or what?"

"Not so fast," Slade answered. He pointed to a small restaurant across the street from the bank. "What say we get us somethin' to eat first? From there, we can check out the street. You know. See what kind of action is goin' on around here."

"Yeah, something to eat. That's a good idea," Murdock agreed.

"Murdock, anytime we eat, it's a good idea as far as you're concerned," Bill Kelly quipped, tugging on his light brown mustache, and the rest of the men laughed.

"Well, I tell you, Kelly, I ain't seen you turn down too many meals yourself," Murdock countered, and the men laughed again.

Tying their horses in front of the restaurant, the riders went inside and ordered ham, eggs, biscuits, and fried potatoes. Their food came, and to anyone watching who had not seen their faces adorning wanted posters, they appeared merely to be five friends lingering over a meal for some friendly conversation.

Shortly after two o'clock, the five men left the restaurant. Kelly and Murdock then rode to the north end of town and Slim trotted to the south end, while Slade and Silverthorn casually walked their horses across the street and hitched them directly in front of the bank. For a few minutes they stood at the door; then, suddenly, the other three men came riding back from either end of town at a full gallop, shooting and whooping loudly, and scattering the terrified bystanders. With the citizens' attention diverted from the bank, Slade and Silverthorn smiled at each other and rushed into the bank.

"Put your hands up!" the outlaw leader shouted gruffly the moment they stepped inside.

The two women customers screamed, while one male customer shouted out in anger, only to be clubbed down by the butt of Silverthorn's pistol.

"Everyone keep quiet in here," Silverthorn commanded. "We'll do all the talkin'."

"You," Slade ordered the bank teller nearest the vault, "start emptyin' out that safe."

The middle-aged bank teller put his hand on the door but then, to Slade's surprise, abruptly slammed it shut.

"That didn't do you no good," Slade snarled. "You're just gonna have to open it again."

"I can't," the teller replied, a self-satisfied look on his moon-shaped face. "It has a time lock."

"A time lock? What the hell does that mean?"

"It means it's impossible for anyone to open it until eight o'clock tomorrow morning," the teller said. He smiled triumphantly. "This is one bank you won't be robbing, today, Mr. Zeke Slade."

"Damn your hide!" Slade growled angrily. Aiming his revolver at the defiant teller, he pulled the trigger and shot the man in the chest.

Eyes widening, the teller gasped, fell against the front of the vault and then slid down to a sitting position. Within a few seconds he was dead.

"Empty the cash drawer and let's get the hell out of here," Slade ordered, and Silverthorn began scooping the loose bills into a sack.

A young office boy, unnoticed by either Slade or Silverthorn, managed to crawl through the back room and out the back door. Once clear of the bank, he ran through the alley out to the main street, shouting, "The bank is being robbed! The bank is being robbed!"

The townspeople suddenly recognized the great show of gunplay for the ruse it was and began arming themselves. Ducking behind barrels and crates, men started firing at the three mounted outlaws. They immediately began firing back, and Luther Murdock felled one man as he rose up from behind a crate to get off a shot from his rifle. The man screamed and clutched his shoulder, then fell behind his cover.

Turning their horses to and fro, making themselves moving targets and therefore harder to hit, Murdock, Kelly, and Hawkins waited with obvious impatience for their cohorts to emerge from the bank. They fired off shot after shot, keeping the townsmen busy protecting their own lives. Occasionally one of the defenders got off a shot of his own, but no bullets struck any of the outlaws.

Slade and Silverthorn rushed out the front door of the bank, with the gang leader holding the money sack in one hand and his revolver in the other. They stopped in their tracks at the sight of the battle taking place twenty yards down the street.

"Damn it, Slade, I knew that was too much shootin'

goin' on to just be our boys!" Silverthorn shouted over the din.

Seeing the men come out of the bank, the citizens of Theresa swarmed to the building, ready for them. "Hold it! You ain't goin' nowhere!" a middle-aged townsman called, a deep frown on his pudgy face. At almost the same time he yelled, he fired his revolver. His bullet missed the outlaws and punched through the front window of the bank. Another man then fired a shot, and his bullet went through Jim Silverthorn's top hat.

"Let's go, let's go!" Slade yelled, shooting back as they ran toward their horses.

From the restaurant in which the men had eaten a few minutes earlier, a citizen, food stains spattered on the front of his shirt, appeared with a shotgun. He let go a blast, but the gun was loaded only with a light bird shot, and his pellets merely peppered the outlaws without penetrating their skin. Another man with a shotgun fired, and the front window of the bank came crashing down.

A man then killed Bill Kelly's horse, but the outlaw merely leapt out of the saddle, leaving his dead animal in the dirt, and ran toward the nearest hitch rail. The many horses left tied by their owners all along the street were spooked by all the gunfire, and they reared and pulled against their restraints.

Kelly grabbed the one nearest him and swung into the saddle as the horse's owner started forward in protest, shouting, "That's my horse!"

"You won't be needin' it no more," Kelly retorted, shooting the man between the eyes from nearly point-blank range. The bullet came out the back of the man's skull and imbedded itself in the dusty street just before the man flopped onto the same spot, his unseeing eyes open in surprise.

With all of them now mounted, the robbers galloped toward the south end of town, but in an attempt to stop them, several men rolled a wagon out into the middle of the dusty street and tipped it over, barricading the way. They then gathered behind it, rifles held at the ready.

"What the hell? What do we do now, Slade?" Slim Hawkins yelled.

"This way!" Slade shouted back, and he reined his mount around, spinning it toward the large plate-glass window fronting a dressmaking shop. He urged his horse forward, and the animal leapt through the window, shattering the glass with an enormous crashing sound and clearing the way for the other four horses that followed close behind.

There were a number of women in the shop, including one being fitted for a new dress. Covering her half-naked, corsetted body with her arms, she and the other ladies screamed in terror as they made a mad dash to get out of the way. The horses clattered and skidded across the wooden floor, then ran through the back door and into an open field behind the store. It was a brilliant move on Slade's part, for none of the townspeople were yet mounted, and by the time they had reached their horses and come around the edge of town, the bank robbers had completely disappeared into the timbered hills.

Zeke Slade, Wyoming's most wanted outlaw, had struck again.

Chapter One

Although it was late at night, the campfire still burned brightly, casting its glow over Zeke Slade and the four members of his gang who were gathered around it, basking in its warmth. They were finally eating their meager supper of beans and coffee, the rich aroma of which permeated the air.

The men were not dressed in standard trail gear. In fact, they were dressed in no particular way that would classify them or identify them as belonging to a certain occupation, for they had chosen their clothes for availability rather than style. Slade, at forty-one the oldest of the group, wore a gray, misshapen Stetson stained with sweat and oil from his lank dark hair. Over his red flannel shirt and denim trousers he wore a brown tweed jacket that seemed more appropriate to a fireplace than the campfire he was staring at angrily with his piercing dark eyes.

Jim Silverthorn's trousers had once belonged to a gentleman's formal evening ensemble—which did not mean that Silverthorn was a gentleman or that he himself had ever dressed so elegantly... only that he had bought the trousers for ten cents at a secondhand clothing store. He had also bought, and was presently wearing, a stovepipe hat, having admired the one Abraham Lincoln had worn in photographs he had seen.

Slim Hawkins wore a brightly colored Mexican serape, not as a mark of his heritage, but for the warmth it provided. Bill Kelly, who had deserted the army some three years earlier, still wore the blue trousers of a cavalry trooper, and the hat on his head was an old army-issue kepi. Luther Murdock was the only one wearing clothes appropriate to the situation—a buckskin jacket, denim trousers, and a green plaid shirt.

However, though the men were dressed in a hodge-podge of clothes, they were unified by several elements: all wore guns, all were rough and hard-looking, they seldom shaved, and they bathed even more rarely.

"How much money did we get from that bank back there?" Kelly asked.

"I ain't counted it exactly," Slade answered, lifting a spoonful of beans to his mouth, then eating noisily. "Silverthorn, you was the one who scooped it into the sack. What would you make it to be?"

"Not as much as it could've been," Silverthorn grumbled, drumming his spoon angrily on the side of his tin plate. "What really makes me mad is that teller closin' the vault door like he did. Who'd a thought a bank in a two-bit town like Theresa'd have a time lock! No tellin' how much money was in that safe." He shook his head. "Little bastard deserved that bullet Zeke put in.his chest. I don't reckon we got any more than five hundred dollars from the cash drawer."

"Five hundred?" Slim yelped. "You mean to tell me we had a shoot-out with half the town, killed a few of 'em, and it was all for no more'n five hundred dollars?"

"That's about the size of it," Slade snapped.

Silverthorn took off his top hat, then held it out for the others to contemplate. "Who'd of thought the whole town'd fight so damn hard over five hundred measly dollars?" he asked. He put his hand up inside the high crown of the hat, then stuck a finger through the hole and wiggled it at the others. "Lookee here, I damn near got my head blowed off—and for what? My share don't hardly come to a hundred dollars."

"Sometimes folks fight hardest when they ain't got much to protect," the gang leader muttered. His dark eyes glowed red in the reflected light as he looked at his cohort and then gestured with his spoon at the man's unfinished pan of food. "Hey, Silverthorn, you gonna eat them beans or not?"

"You wanna know the truth of it, Slade, I'm gettin' goddamn sick of beans," Silverthorn replied, handing his plate over to Slade, who scraped the beans off into his own plate.

Pouring himself a cup of coffee, Slim Hawkins hunkered down into his serape and remarked, "Yeah, Slade, I ain't a complainin' man, but the next time we hold us up a bank, let's make sure it ain't got one of them time-lock safes in it, okay?"

"Have a little patience, Slim. This job was just to get us a little operatin' money is all," Slade replied, a smug expression on his face. "Truth is, I got us a deal planned now that's gonna bring us enough money so's we can quit if we want to." His eyes gleaming, he paused for effect and then asked, "How does a hundred thousand dollars to divvy up sound to you boys?"

"A hundred thousand dollars?" Slim shouted. "Whooee, I didn't even know there was that much money in the world!" He tugged thoughtfully on his dark mustache and then asked, "Where're we gonna find that kind of money?"

"Remember when I told all you boys that I was

gonna make you rich one day?" Slade queried. "Well, that day's near to hand."

"One hundred thousand or five hundred dollars— what difference does it make if a man has to hide out in the mountains all the time and eat nothin' but beans?" Silverthorn complained, tossing his empty plate onto the ground.

"Silverthorn, you'd bitch if you was hung with a new rope," Kelly snickered, and they all laughed.

"I reckon we'll find out the truth of that someday," Slim observed, "seein' as we're all probably gonna end up doin' a little dance for the hangman."

"I'd rather be hung than spend any more time in prison," Zeke Slade rejoined. "There's some things worse than dyin', and bein' in prison is one of 'em."

Unknown to the band of outlaws, they were being observed and overheard. Just beyond the circle of firelight, Nate Yeager was sneaking among the boulders that half ringed the campsite, being careful not to make any noise.

Tall, lean, and muscular, Nate was only twenty-six, but he had seen his share of hard times, and his handsome face and clear blue eyes reflected a maturity beyond his years. His sandy hair was matted with sweat, and he sported a four-day stubble—not because he was growing a beard, but because it had been that long since he had had the opportunity to shave. Like the men in the camp, Nate Yeager was armed and rawhide-tough. Unlike them, however, he had a sense of values and knew right from wrong—and he was there now because he intended to correct a wrong.

Although it was the middle of May, spring came late to Wyoming's Rattlesnake Mountain Range, and that night was particularly cold. Nate was wearing only a cotton shirt, having left his long, tan duster rolled up on the back of his saddle for fear of tripping on it. He shivered as he envied the fire that Zeke Slade and his men were enjoying and blew on the palms of his hands in a futile effort to warm them.

Having moved down closer, hiding behind a large boulder, he had been able to hear what was being said in the camp, and he had to agree with the last comment. Being in prison was worse than dying . . . which was why he had been willing to risk his life a few days ago in order to escape from the territorial prison.

Never, even in his most terrible nightmare, had Nate Yeager expected to wind up in jail, but that was exactly where he had spent the last two years, after being framed by the very man he was staring at—Zeke Slade—who had also killed his brother, Cole. Nate thought about those two years in prison—the dehumanization, the awful food, and especially the abandoned hopes and lost souls of those who were in there with him, and as he circled the campsite, he recalled all too vividly the events leading up to his imprisonment.

He and his older brother had been building a ranch and working hard to fulfill their shared dream. In order to help make ends meet until the ranch became self-supporting, Nate had taken on an extra job. While Cole stayed home and tended the ranch, Nate drove a stagecoach for the Wyoming Express Company.

Nate had heard of Zeke Slade—as had just about everyone else in Wyoming Territory. Slade and his gang of cutthroats had moved across the countryside like a prairie fire, leaving a string of murders and robberies in their wake. But Nate was not a lawman, so Zeke Slade barely occupied his thoughts.

However, that was all to change.

Shortly after Nate had completed what was to be his last stagecoach run, he had hurried home to the ranch to help his brother with the spring roundup of cattle. It had been a good winter, with very few losses to wolves or weather, and a number of calves had been born. At long last it looked as if the two brothers were about to turn the ranch into a profitable operation, which meant Nate could give up his stagecoach job and spend full time on the ranch. And it also meant that Cole would be able to ask the daughter of a neighboring rancher to marry him.

There was no such girl on the horizon for Nate. Though he had never said anything—and never would because his older brother had staked the claim first— Nate did not think he could ever be interested in a woman unless he could find one exactly like Cole's girl. She was beautiful and high-spirited, and she knew horses and cattle as well as any man. Nate thought that she was perfect and would be the perfect rancher's wife. Unfortunately that rancher would be Cole, not he.

For two days, the brothers had searched all the draws and canyons of their ranch, making certain that they rounded up every last calf for branding. After they had finished, Nate and Cole decided to go into town for a little relaxation in celebration of their newfound status as "gentlemen" ranchers.

"Well, ranchers anyway," Cole had agreed, a broad grin splitting his ruggedly handsome face. "I'm not all that certain about the gentleman part."

"That's the part that I *am* sure about," Nate had retorted. "Ma taught us to be gentlemen—she never taught us to be ranchers."

"Maybe Pa would have," Cole had mused.

"I often wonder what he was like. Do you remember him, Cole?" the younger brother had queried.

"I can remember him coming home once during the war," Cole had answered, a sad smile on his face. "I remember his sword. . . . I thought it was the most wonderful thing I had ever seen. He let me hold it. I must've killed a hundred Rebels with it—at least, in my imagination."

"I don't remember any of that."

His older brother had softly replied, "No way you could. You were only two years old when Pa was killed at Shiloh. I was six."

They had continued on toward town when suddenly Nate's horse threw a shoe, and the two men had been forced to stop. Cole had affectionately scolded, "I told you the day before yesterday that that shoe looked loose. Some rancher you are, little brother. You can't even keep your horse shod." Grinning, he had continued, "Never mind. I've got some tools in my saddlebag. Get down from there and we'll take care of it."

The brothers had no sooner gotten off their horses to look at the problem when five men had come galloping hard over the ridge. The man in the lead had pointed at them and then headed directly toward the young ranchers.

As the riders reined to an abrupt halt, Cole had greeted, "Howdy."

"Havin' some trouble?" one of the riders—a man with a long, deeply hollowed face and a large handlebar mustache— had asked, swinging down from his horse. The man's four friends had then dismounted as well.

"Nothing serious," Cole had replied lightly. "Just a loose shoe is all." He had squinted at the men. "Don't believe I ever met any of you gents. You just come into the territory?"

"Yeah, we're lookin' for work."

Cole had shrugged. "I'm afraid you're too late. Spring roundup's over, so I doubt there's much work around any of the ranches right now. Maybe you fellas can find something in one of the towns—at a livery or stageline, perhaps."

Nodding, Nate had suggested, "Matter of fact, the stageline in Buffalo is looking for a hostler."

"Where's this Buffalo?"

"Just north of here, maybe five or six miles," Cole had answered. "We're going there now to have a couple of beers. You're welcome to ride along with us." He then laughed. "That is, if my brother ever gets that shoe fixed."

Ignoring his brother's jibe, the younger rancher had lifted the horse's foot and then leaned over to examine the hoof more closely. Suddenly Cole had yelled, "What the hell?" Nate had looked up just as one of the riders slammed the butt of his pistol down on Nate's head. At the same time that he had felt a sharp stab of pain, Nate also thought he heard a loud popping noise, but then everything quickly went black.

"Get up," someone had demanded.

Opening his eyes, Nate had found that he was lying on his stomach, with his face in the dirt. He had no idea where he was or why he was lying on the ground, though he sensed there were several people standing around, looking down at him.

His head throbbed and his brain seemed to be shrouded in fog. Who were they, and why were they there? Why was *he* there?

The young rancher had tried to get up, but everything started spinning so badly that he nearly passed out again. He was conscious of a terrible pain on the top of his head, and when he had reached up and touched the spot gingerly, his fingers came away sticky with blood. Holding his fingers in front of his eyes, he had stared at them in surprise.

"What happened?" he had finally asked, his tongue thick, as though he had been drinking too much.

"There was a fallin' out among thieves, that's what

happened," came a gruff voice. "The other boys turned on you two, emptied your bank sacks, and took the money with 'em."

Utterly confused, Nate had muttered, "I don't know what you're talking about."

"No sense in tryin' to get away with that line of bull," the man had said. "You're the one we want, all right. And just 'cause you wound up without any of the money, it don't make you no less guilty. You're gonna hang, fella. Your partner would hang, too, if your friends hadn't already killed him. Now, are you gonna get up, or am I gonna have to tie a rope around your feet and drag you all the way back to Banner?"

"Who are you?" Nate had asked, managing to make it to his knees and looking up. He had been right in sensing that there were several people around him. In addition to the one who was obviously in charge—a burly man of about forty-five with a deeply lined face— there were six more men glaring at him and brandishing an arsenal of weapons ranging from revolvers to rifles to shotguns—all of which were pointing at him.

"I'm the town marshal from Banner," the burly man had answered, holding open his jacket to expose the tin star pinned to his shirt, "and these here men are my deputies. I reckon you and your friends figured you could rob our bank 'cause we're so small, but you got yourselves another think comin'. Get up."

"I don't know what you're talking about," Nate had repeated and started to get to his feet when he suddenly noticed his brother. Cole was lying on his back, his arms flopped out on either side of him.

"Cole!" he screamed. "Oh, my God!" Seeing the ugly black hole between his brother's eyes, Nate had hurried to him. He had put his hand on Cole's neck to check for a pulse, but before he even touched him, he had known his brother was dead. Nate had instantly felt a profound sense of sorrow and loneliness.

"Is that this fella's name? Cole?"

"Yes. Cole Yeager," Nate had choked out. "He's my brother. I'm Nate Yeager."

"Well, Nate Yeager, I'm arrestin' you for the murderin' and bank robbin' you and the others done up in Banner," the marshal had announced. One of the other men had grabbed Nate roughly, twisted his hands behind his back and then shackled them together.

"Help him on his horse," the marshal had ordered. "And then pick up them empty bank bags. We'll be needin' 'em as evidence."

Roughly put onto his horse, Nate Yeager had protested, "Marshal, please listen to me! My brother and I didn't hold up any bank! We've been working on our ranch for the last two days! We were just heading into Buffalo to celebrate finishing our spring roundup when we were jumped by five men!"

"Uh huh," the lawman had answered, unimpressed. "You got any witnesses can verify any of this tale?"

"Well, no," Nate had admitted. "We've been out on the range, and we don't have any hands. There are . . . *were* just the two of us."

"Too bad you ain't got no witnesses, Yeager, 'cause I do. At least half a dozen of 'em. And they'll everyone of 'em swear they seen you and your brother ridin' out of town with Zeke Slade."

Nate's eyes had widened with surprise as he suddenly realized who the five riders were. "Zeke Slade? Well, I'll be damned. *That's* who that was!" Shaking his head angrily, the young rancher had insisted, "Well, your witnesses are wrong—dead wrong!"

"Mister, *I'm* one of them witnesses," the marshal had rejoined emphatically, pointing to his chest. "So don't you go tellin' me what I did and what I didn't see." He then pointed at Nate's chest, adding, "I remember them plaid shirts you and your brother's wearin' like as if there was a picture of 'em drawn on my eyeballs."

Bewildered, Nate had glanced down at the shirt he wore, then at the shirt his brother was wearing, and he had wondered if he were going mad. They were not the shirts they had put on when they had left the ranch! Gasping sharply, he had then remembered that two of Slade's cohorts had been wearing shirts just like these.

Squeezing his eyes shut, then opening them, as if somehow that would bring things into focus, Nate had reconstructed a picture of what had happened. Apparently Zeke Slade had used Nate and Cole to buy some time from the posse that had given chase after the bank robbery. They had knocked out Nate, killed Cole and then changed shirts with them. To enhance the frame, they had even left a couple of empty bank sacks.

"Marshal, you're making a big mistake!" Nate had desperately declared.

"No, friend," the lawman had responded. "The only ones who made any mistakes around here was you and your brother. And you boys made three of 'em." Ticking them off on his fingers, he had enumerated: "Your first one was in pickin' a bank in my town to rob; your second was in trustin' a man like Zeke Slade—you can see where that got you; and your third was in gettin' yourself caught. Now, let's go."

. "What about my brother? You aren't just going to leave him here?"

"I'll send word to the undertaker in Buffalo to come out and get him." Smirking, he had added, "Don't worry. He ain't goin' nowhere."

Nate had not even been allowed to attend his brother's burial. At the time of the funeral, the young rancher was attending his own trial. Officials of the

Wyoming Express Company as well as Sheriff Clint Townsend of Buffalo had testified on Nate's behalf, but the case hinged on the accounts of the six eyewitnesses, all good citizens of Banner... and Banner was where the trial was held.

Other than the "good character" testimony provided by his friends, Nate had had absolutely no defense. The only thing that had saved him from hanging was the testimony of several of the witnesses who believed the bullet that killed the deputy had been fired by Zeke Slade himself. Nate had been found innocent of murder but guilty of armed robbery, and he was sentenced to twenty years of hard labor in the territorial prison.

Nate Yeager had been a model prisoner for two years. Then, a week ago, a lawyer had ridden to the prison to talk to his client. After tying his horse outside the warden's office, the visitor had checked his pistol with the warden's clerk and hung his hat and the long tan duster he had worn for the ride from Buffalo on a coatrack in the warden's office. The young prisoner, who had been mopping the office floor, had watched it all.

Minutes later, purely by happenstance, a fight had broken out among some of the prisoners. From all over the prison, guards had rushed to the scene to break it up before it spread into a riot. The warden and his clerk had also hurried out into the yard, and the lawyer had followed along, just to watch the action.

Seeing that the lawyer's horse, gun, duster, and hat were unattended, Nate had quickly put the mop down, strapped on the gun, slipped into the duster, pulled the hat low over his face and then mounted the lawyer's horse and ridden out the front gate just as if he had had every right to do so. The guards at the gate had been so busy looking back toward the yard at all the excitement that they had barely glanced at Nate as he rode out.

It was pure luck rather than good tracking skills that had brought Nate Yeager to Zeke Slade's campsite. Traveling by night so as to avoid any posse that might be out looking for him, Nate had seen the glow of Slade's campfire and cautiously approached. He had been expecting to find some cowboys in the middle of a roundup bedded down for the night, not the notorious outlaw and his gang discussing their last robbery and planning their next.

Now that he had found Slade, he was not exactly certain what he was going to do with him. There had been a time, during his first five or six months in prison, when he had been so filled with rage, all he could think of was avenging his brother's death—but now what he wanted was to prove his innocence. He was not sure how capturing Zeke Slade would do that—his idea was vaguely formed at best—but he felt that if he could capture him and turn him over to the authorities, he could force the outlaw to clear him.

Deciding to try to improve his position to get the drop on the gang, Nate moved down through the boulders. Suddenly his foot dislodged a large rock, and it tumbled down noisily.

"What the hell was that?" Zeke Slade yelled, his pan of beans flying as he stood up quickly, his gun in his hand in an instant. "Silverthorn, douse them flames!" he ordered. Coffee was immediately thrown on the fire, and it sizzled and smoked as it went out.

Fearing discovery, Nate started to scramble over the boulder-strewn ground to where he had left his horse.

"There! I saw something!" someone shouted, and the shout was followed almost immediately by a shot.

The others began firing as well, and as they fired, the flames from the muzzles of their guns lit up the dark like flashes of summer lightning. Bullets sparked off the boulders all around Nate, and one ricocheted so close to his ear that he could feel the sharp puff of air at its passing. It ran through his mind that he suddenly knew how his father must have felt during the war, with enemy fire striking all around him. He only hoped he would not end up the same way—dead with a bullet in his skull.

"After him!" one of the bandits shouted.

Another shot was fired, and it hit a rock by Nate's feet, digging out a piece of the rock and slamming it painfully into the young prisoner's leg. He was thankful for the thick, sturdy denim cloth that protected his skin; otherwise, the shard would have penetrated as though it were a slug.

He neared the place where he had left his horse when another slug whizzed by his head. Reflexively leaping to one side, the ground where he had been standing a moment before was suddenly struck by a bullet, and a piece of sod went flying into the air.

Running nimbly, having occasionally to fling himself flat on the ground, Nate finally made it to his horse. Not until he was mounted did he send a shot back toward his pursuers, using the flame bursts from their guns as targets. He then urged the horse forward, but it was the mount he had stolen from the lawyer, and the lawyer had obviously selected it for gentleness and ease of handling, not for its agility or quickness. If he had been riding a responsive quarterhorse, he might have escaped into the darkness. Instead, the horse, already frightened by the gunshots and by demands being made of him, balked and then refused to make a jump.

Nate was panicky. He could tell by their voices, getting steadily and increasingly louder, that the outlaws were drawing closer, and they kept up their barrage of shots as they approached. Suddenly the young prisoner felt, rather than heard, a bullet hit his horse. The animal shuddered once and then went down. Leaping quickly from the saddle to keep from being pinned underneath, Nate hit the ground painfully, crying out as he fell.

With a shout of triumph, believing they had him, his pursuers pressed forward, but Nate rolled on the ground, trying to keep his visibility to a minimum. Suddenly the ground gave way as he came to the edge of a steep cliff that was barely evident in the light of the cloud-covered moon, and he cautiously started descending. Finding purchase for his hands and feet wherever he could—in crevices, scrub trees, and brush—he worked his way down and soon reached the bottom, some one hundred feet below. The moon came out from behind a cloud for a moment, and Nate discerned a well-used animal trail and started running. Within minutes, he could no longer hear Zeke Slade or his men.

He kept going for another quarter hour. Finally, assuming he was safe, the exhausted young man crawled into the middle of a thick stand of bushes and then curled up and went to sleep.

When dawn broke a few hours later, Nate Yeager took stock of his situation. He had managed to escape the outlaw band, but all of his gear was back with his fallen horse. He had nothing—not even a canteen—and now not only was wanted by the law, but he was in the middle of nowhere and had lost all track of his quarry.

With a sigh, he stood and began the long trek down from the mountains.

Shannon McBride opened her eyes and looked through the window of the railroad car and then smiled with pleasure. The dawn sky was streaked with various shades of red, gold, and purple, and she had almost forgotten how wonderful the sunrises and sunsets could be in Wyoming. Toying with a lock of her long dark hair, she lay in her berth listening to the rhythmic clack the wheels made on the tracks and enjoying the patterns and colors of the breathtakingly beautiful, ever-changing sky.

No! Shannon suddenly reprimanded herself, her light blue eyes flashing and her fair skin flushing, *I won't enjoy this!* Angrily turning her head away from the window, she stared at the heavy green curtain that covered her berth. She refused to allow herself to be seduced by the rugged beauty of this land, for she knew that this country had little to offer other than brutal winters, blistering summers, hard work, and heartbreak.

Shannon reminded herself of the cruel tricks Wyoming had already played on her. Two years ago she had suffered a personal tragedy so traumatic that her father had sent her away to a women's school in Boston. At the time, she had not wanted to go, but her father had insisted, and the experience had turned into an awakening for Shannon.

The school she had attended was in the forefront of women's education, and she had come to regard herself in an entirely new light. Additionally, she got a glimpse of a world that she had not even known existed: She discovered great libraries that contained more books than she could read in a hundred lifetimes; she visited museums to view some of the world's greatest art treasures; she attended concerts where the music was so beautiful it could rival the Heavenly Hosts; she saw plays and ballets performed by the foremost artists of the day; and she attended lectures given by the most learned men in the world.

Boston had indoor plumbing and gas lights, steam heat and elevators, hospitals where medical miracles were being performed, and even telephones. After two years, Shannon had come to believe that Boston was the only place to be, and she wondered why anyone would ever want to live in a place like Wyoming.

Then she had received a letter from her father explaining that a very difficult winter had dealt the ranch such serious financial setbacks that he could no longer afford to keep her in the school. Stoically, Shannon looked upon that as but one more of the penalties Wyoming extracted from those people crazy enough or stubborn enough to choose to live there.

In the letter, Shannon's father asked her to please come back home, and this Shannon was doing. But in her own mind she was going home only long enough to convince her father to sell his ranch and return East with her. In Boston, her father could live quite comfortably for the rest of his life just on the money he could get from selling the ranch.

On the other side of the heavy green curtain that covered her berth and afforded her some privacy, Shannon heard the porter walking through the cars, announcing that breakfast was now being served in the dining car. With a deep sigh, she roused herself and struggled into her clothes; then she climbed down from the berth and hurried to the end of the car to the washroom.

"Ah, dear, there you are!" Nell Gentry, a smile lighting up her strikingly lovely face, greeted Shannon as she arrived in the dining car a few minutes later. The sunlight streaming through the window glinted on Nell's auburn hair, making it look like burnished copper. Nell's eight-year-old son, Tad, hurried around to pull the chair out for Shannon as she joined her friends.

"Thank you, Tad. What a wonderful young gentleman you are," Shannon enthused as she gathered the long skirt of her green silk frock around her to sit.

"Today's the day, Miss McBride," Tad remarked, ignoring the compliment. "We get home today!"

"Not quite, Tad," Nell reminded her son. "Remember, we still have quite a long stagecoach ride ahead of us."

"Yes, but at least we're in Wyoming," Tad countered. "I'm really glad to be back. I hated Philadelphia."

Shannon laughed and shook her head. "So here are the two of us. You can hardly wait to get back, and I wish I didn't have to return."

Coincidentally, Shannon had run across Nell and her son as they were changing trains in Omaha. Before she had left Wyoming, Shannon had known the Gentrys, for Nell and her husband had run a small hotel and restaurant in Buffalo, Wyoming, which was the town nearest her father's ranch. Then Nell's husband died last year, and her sister, who lived in Philadelphia, insisted that Nell and Tad come to live with her and her husband. Closing up her hotel, Nell had rented out the lobby to the Wyoming Express Company to use as their depot. Then she had packed up her clothes and some personal belongings and took her son East.

It had not worked out. Nell missed having her own home, and she missed her friends. But most of all, she missed Wyoming. Finally, when she could no longer resist the desire to return, she said a tearful farewell to her sister and bought train tickets back to Wyoming.

When Nell and Shannon had met on the train in Omaha, they immediately renewed their friendship. They proved to be wonderful company for one another during the long train ride, even though there was quite a difference in age between the two women, for Shannon was in her early twenties while Nell was in her mid-thirties. The physical differences between them were equally as great— the one brunette and dark complected and the other redheaded and fair—though each woman was exceptionally lovely in her own way.

The two women chatted cheerily through breakfast; then Shannon noticed that the boy had eaten very little. "Tad, I don't believe it," the young brunette joshed. "You, the world's champion pancake eater, are passing up your last morning's stack of them?"

"I guess I'm just not very hungry, Miss McBride," Tad answered.

Nell put a solicitous hand on her son's forehead. "I don't know, Shannon, he was complaining of a stomachache during the night," she explained. "It may have been something he ate."

"Yes, or perhaps it's train sickness," Shannon suggested. "I've observed that it can sometimes occur even if you've been riding for several days with no previous ill effects."

"Yes," Nell agreed, nodding, "perhaps so." She smiled. "If that's what it is, he'll certainly have the opportunity to recover soon enough. The conductor told me a short while ago that we'll be arriving in Medicine Bow in about an hour, so we'll finally be done riding trains." She studied Shannon for a moment and then suggested, "You know, my dear, you might want to reconsider your dress. While it's most becoming, and I do so admire the beautiful lacework on the collar and cuffs, it seems a bit . . . well, a bit too civilized for a stagecoach ride."

The young woman looked down at her dress and then at the sensible blue wool shirtwaist with buttons up the front that Nell was wearing. Shannon touched a napkin to her lips and smiled at her table companions. "Well, you are absolutely right. I don't know what I was thinking." Then she laughed ruefully and declared, "I guess after two years of getting used to city transportation, I'd put out of my mind how rough-and-tumble stagecoaches are. Therefore, I had better get back to my berth to change my dress, then gather my belongings and get ready to disembark."

"Disembark?" Tad asked.

Shannon smiled. "It means get off the train."

The boy made a face and then admonished, "Why didn't you say that? Why did you use such a fancy word?"

"Tad!" his mother scolded.

"No, Nell, he's quite right," Shannon said. "I shouldn't be so . . ." She started to say "pretentious" but then realized that the word itself was pretentious. So she smiled and said instead, "fancy. I'll see you before we get off."

"That can't come fast enough for me!" Tad exclaimed.

Standing, Shannon McBride merely smiled thinly and then headed back to her berth. *As far as I'm concerned,* she thought to herself, *this train could take all the time in the world to get to Wyoming, and it wouldn't bother me in the least.*

Chapter Two

In the Boar's Head Saloon in Medicine Bow, Wyoming, the gambler took his beer over to a table and then sat down. A thin layer of tobacco smoke hanging just beneath the ceiling drifted and curled through the room, then collected in a small cloud above the man's table. Noticing it, he wondered if it were some portent of doom; then he shook his head and laughed inwardly. *You're not getting superstitious in your old age, are you, Trey?* he asked himself.

In his early forties, Trey Farnsworth was handsome in a rather tired and jaded way. But unlike most of the other men in the saloon, the gambler was clean—in fact, almost fastidiously so—and his dark hair and equally dark eyes were mirrored by the fashionable, even elegant black clothes he always wore. There was also an air about him, a way he had of being detached from everything and everyone . . . even himself.

He picked up a deck of cards with hands that clearly had never done a hard day's labor, spread the cards out, and adroitly turned the entire deck over by passing a card back across the top. After that he let the pasteboards waterfall from hand to hand, his long fingers working so adeptly that it almost appeared as if magic were at work. Then he shuffled them and began dealing an imaginary poker game, for there was no one else at the table to receive the cards.

He had been in Medicine Bow for two weeks now, and he had been so successful at the poker tables that he could no longer find anyone to play with him. With a sigh, he turned over all the hands, noting the fall of certain cards, then picked them up, reshuffled, and dealt again.

A train whistle sounded outside, breaking the silence of the room, and the bartender pulled out his pocketwatch and looked at it rather pointedly, almost as if he were responsible for the arrivals and departures of the Union Pacific trains. At the same time, a couple of men at the bar nodded at each other, passing a silent signal between them. Suddenly Trey Farnsworth heard the double click of a revolver being cocked, and he felt the cold metal of a gun barrel pressed against the back of his head.

"Mr. Gamblin' Man," a deep voice hissed from behind him. "You're just too damned good with them there cards for the likes of Medicine Bow."

Trey tensed and laid the cards down. He kept his hands facedown and in full view on the table in what he hoped was a gesture that clearly indicated that he would not try anything. Clearing his throat, he asked, "Is skill against the law in this town?"

"Your kind of skill is," the unseen man behind him replied. "Now, we ain't exactly callin' you a cheater, you understand, 'cause if that's what you've been doin', there ain't none of us been able to catch you at it. Rest assured that if we had, we'd be stringin' you up about now, instead of doin' what we're doin'."

"I see," Trey said, able to breathe a bit easier. If they were not going to lynch him, then it seemed less

likely that this man would pull the trigger and kill him
by shooting him. Calmly, he began picking his cards up
from the table. "I take it, then, that I am being run out
of town?"

"That you are, mister," the man replied. "I reckon
you just heard the train whistle?"

"I did."

"That train'll be standin' at the depot for forty-five
minutes; then it heads on west. There'll be a stage
leavin' the depot 'bout the same time, headin' north.
We don't much care which form of transport it is you
choose, but you're gonna be on one of 'em."

Trey grinned laconically and straightened his string
tie. "Well, since I've about exhausted my welcome
along the Union Pacific route, I'm going to have to start
looking for virgin territory. Therefore, I guess I'll take
the stagecoach north. May I at least go over to the hotel
and get my bag?"

"No need for that, Gamblin' Man. We got it for
you." So saying, the man dropped a leather valise
beside Trey's chair.

"May I turn around, please? I would like to see the
composition of this farewell committee."

"Sure, go ahead, turn around," the man agreed.
"Ain't none of us got any reason to hide from the likes of
you." He laughed, adding, "Aside from which, ain't no
way you'd be able to walk out of the saloon without
turnin' around— and you sure as hell are gonna be
walkin' outta here."

When Trey turned, he saw that there were at least
six men with the spokesman. He recognized every one
of them—and had in fact played cards with each of
them.

"Ah, George," he said to the man holding the gun.
"Is it because you couldn't fill an inside straight that
you decided to take your frustrations out in this way?

And you, Phil"—he shook his head slowly, berating the man—"breaking a pair of jacks to go for a flush when the pair alone would have won the hand. Oh, and we mustn't forget Charley, a man who thinks bluster and bluff will compensate for an inadequate hand."

"That's enough of all that," a well-dressed man said. Trey recognized him as Marcus Pendarrow, a businessman who had played often—and lost often. "You're trying to get us to fight among ourselves," Pendarrow snapped, "but your tricks won't work. We are men of resolve, and we intend to see that you leave town."

Trey dropped his cards in his jacket pocket and then leaned down to pick up his bag.

"Well, then, you gentlemen of. . . resolve . . . I bid you good day," he said, nodding graciously at his send-off committee. Standing, he strode quickly across the room, pushed through the batwing doors, and stepped out into the afternoon sun. He stood there for a moment, blinking at the unaccustomed brightness, and then headed for the depot a block away. This was a routine procedure with him by now. Medicine Bow was not the first town he had ever been asked to leave.

As the train rattled to a stop at the Medicine Bow station, Nell Gentry and Shannon McBride gazed out the window, each lost in her own thoughts. Both women looked out at the same scene: a station platform stacked with crates and boxes and, beyond that, a dirt street and a scattering of perhaps thirty low, unpainted, clapboard buildings. But though both saw the same things, they perceived them differently.

To Shannon, this was the exact opposite of the life she had been living and enjoying in Boston, and she resented the injustices that had forced her to return to what she thought of as a godforsaken place. Nell, on the other hand, welcomed the sun-bleached buildings, the dust-covered men and women, and the heat waves radiating off the endless, empty plains. They were old and familiar things to her, and they had tightened their hold so securely around her heart that, seeing them now, she knew she would never leave them again.

The depot was a flurry of activity and noise. On the platform, men yelled at each other as a steel-wheeled cart was rolled up to the baggage car to load and unload suitcases, crates, and mailbags. Here the train also took on water, precipitating a great deal of banging and clanging of tank covers and waterspouts as the engine's reservoir was filled. The fireman kept the fire stoked and the steam going, and the rhythmic opening and closing of the valves as the pressure repeatedly built up and then vented away sounded remarkably like the laborious breathing of some great beast of burden.

In addition to those people manning the depot and the train and the passengers arriving and departing—plus those meeting them or sending them off—dozens of townspeople, to whom the arrival of the train was a major event, crowded the depot. This particular train also corresponded with the arrival and departure of the stagecoach heading north, lending an even more festive air to the occasion.

A few of the more urbane transcontinental passengers, those going on through to San Francisco, got off the train to stretch their legs and have a look around. Standing on the platform, they gawked at the local men lounging against the wall of the depot, their hips adorned with cartridge belts and pistols. The visitors stared unabashedly at the locals, for these were real "cowboys" of the type they had only read about, and they watched closely, waiting for the sudden explosion of temper that might lead to one of the famous gunfights that they presumed occurred regularly in towns like this one.

A few moments later, when a drayman popped his whip with the explosiveness of a pistol shot, several of the easterners jumped. Their eyes wide in fright and fascination, they drew closer together, the better to stay out of the path of any flying projectiles from the gunfight they were sure had broken out.

Laughing softly, Nell remarked to Shannon, "I suppose none of these city slickers have ever heard a bullwhip before."

"I suppose not," Shannon agreed, also laughing. Though she had lived with easterners for the past two years and had even come to regard herself as one of them, she could not help but smirk at their tenderfoot reaction, and she felt a sense of superiority over them.

"Mama, I don't feel very good," Tad suddenly moaned, holding his stomach.

"Oh, dear! I just don't know what's wrong with you," Nell replied, kneeling and putting a hand on her son's cheek. "Why don't you go over there and lie down on that bench, while I get our stage tickets?"

"I'll stay with him until you get the tickets; then I'll get mine," Shannon volunteered.

"Thank you. That's very sweet of you," Nell sighed, standing and drawing her cream-colored shawl tighter around her shoulders, warding off the morning chill.

The ticket office for the stage line was inside the railroad depot. Nell arrived at the door leading into the building at the same time as a man dressed in black. The man smiled graciously, stepped back, and opened the door for her.

"After you, madam," he said.

"Thank you."

Nell bought tickets for herself and Tad to Buffalo; then, head down, she stepped aside to put them in her reticule. As she pulled the drawstring tight, about to head out of the depot, she was surprised to hear the man who had been behind her buy a ticket to the same destination. Turning, she saw that it was the same man who had held open the door.

She smiled at him, asking, "Do you live in Buffalo?" Then she laughed nervously. "I'm sorry. I know it was rude of me to inquire, but I used to live in Buffalo, and now I'm going back home. I was just wondering if we were neighbors."

"I couldn't think of anyone I would rather be neighbors with," the man said, touching the brim of his flat-crowned black hat as he smiled at her. "But the truth is, I'll be visiting your fair town for the first time."

"Oh," Nell murmured. She found the man intriguingly handsome, and the more she talked with him, the more certain she was that she was making a fool of herself. "Well, I, uh, I'm sure you will enjoy it," she remarked diffidently. "If you'll excuse me now, I must see to my son. You see, I'm a widow and—" Nell stopped in mid-sentence and felt her face burning in embarrassment. She wished a pit would open up and swallow her whole. *Why* had she told him she was a widow? How obvious could a person be?

But the man smiled with seemingly genuine pleasure and said, "My name is Trey Farnsworth. May I inquire as to your name?"

"Nell. That is, Nell Gentry."

"Mrs. Gentry, as we'll be traveling companions, and you are without a husband, I do hope you will call on me if you should need any assistance."

"Uh, yes, thank you," Nell mumbled, unable to meet his gaze. "But I'm sure I will have no difficulty."

"Nevertheless, madam, I shall remain at your service."

The redhead nodded and then scurried to the door.

Waiting for Nell to return, Shannon McBride saw a tall, slim young man come out of the depot building.

For a moment she thought she recognized him, and she half stood and raised her hand to call out to him. Then the young man turned his head, enabling Shannon to see him more clearly, and she realized he was not who she thought he was. But then, of course, how could he have been? The person she had thought he might be was dead.

It had taken her a long time to get over the guilt of his death. Not that she was responsible for it—she had had nothing to do with it—but she had been living a lie, never once finding the courage to end it.

They were to have been wed. He thought she loved him—and at one time, she thought so as well. Then she met another, and though propriety and honor would never let her declare that love, nor accept it had it been declared to her, she found that the face of the man in her most troublesome dreams belonged to *this* man, and not to the one she was pledged to marry.

The dilemma was solved for Shannon in the cruelest and most tragic way when her betrothed had died, believing that Shannon's love for him was as strong as his for her. That deceit troubled Shannon far more than she could ever admit to anyone.

Not wanting to think about it, she glanced away from the handsome young cowboy and began talking with Tad Gentry about the impending stagecoach ride.

Inside one of the houses on the other side of town, in the small residential section of Medicine Bow, Sidney Durant stood at the side of his bed, hurriedly packing his suitcase under the watchful eye of his wife, Clara. Taking a shirt from a drawer, Durant unfolded it and then refolded it, making absolutely certain that every crease was in the right place and no new wrinkles were being formed.

A short, thin man in his late thirties, Durant had

blue eyes, brown hair, and a small, closely cropped mustache. He was extremely fastidious looking, a trait even more evidenced by the great care he was taking with his packing.

Suddenly the bedsprings groaned in protest as his wife shifted.

"Sidney?" she called.

"Yes."

"Sidney, look at me."

Obeying, Sidney found that his wife had removed her dress and her undergarments as well, which were hanging from the big brass ball on one side of the headboard. Clara was a very large, relatively plain-looking woman, although some men were particularly partial to her generous shape, with its abundant breasts. Her husband, unfortunately, was not one of those men.

Durant sighed and closed his eyes. "Clara, for God's sake, cover yourself," he muttered in a low, flat voice. "You shouldn't be seen like that. You are positively indecent."

"Naked is the way we all come into the world, Sidney. There's absolutely nothing indecent about it," Clara protested.

"Men and women do not come into this world with fully matured bodies," he countered, his voice cold.

"Perhaps not, but I am your wife—and there is nothing indecent about a man seeing his own wife naked."

"The only time a man should ever see his wife naked is at night—when he can't see her at all," Durant sniffed.

"Don't you love me?"

"Of course I do," he answered without expression or conviction. Looking away from her, he went back to packing his suitcase.

He was aware of Clara's eyes on him, watching his

every movement. Sneaking a glance at her, he found her looking at him with hurt eyes, and after a moment, she opened her mouth to speak.

Hesitantly, she said, "This pains me, but I have to ask it, Sidney: Would you love me if my father wasn't the president of the bank and you weren't his chief clerk?"

"Clara, what kind of a question is that?" Durant demanded, sidestepping an answer. "Why, you degrade yourself—and me—by asking such things."

"I'm sorry, I can't help it," she replied. Her eyes misted over with tears. "Sidney, I realize I am not a very pretty woman. But I could be a good wife to you if you would only let me." Shamelessly, almost pleadingly, she ran her hand down the side of her body, letting it slide over the curve of her hip. "I can be *very* good to you," she added in a sultry tone.

"You are fine, Clara. I have no complaints," he responded, his voice flat and cool. Finally putting his last pair of trousers into the suitcase, he closed it and then buckled it shut.

"How long will you be in Buffalo?" Clara asked with a sigh, clearly giving up the notion of seduction to arouse her husband's interest.

"I don't know," Durant answered as he put his brown pin-striped jacket on and then tugged at the cuffs of his shirt. "Maybe as long as a month . . . or perhaps even longer. Your father has charged me with a very serious responsibility. As you know, this past winter was an extremely hard one in northern Wyoming, and many of the cattlemen were badly hurt. I will be handling a series of emergency loans, which is why I will be carrying a secret shipment of money with me—one of the largest ever transferred by the Medicine Bow Bank."

"Yes, I understand," Clara murmured. Suddenly she smiled and sat up on the bed. "Sidney?"

"Yes, what is it?"

"What if I would come to Buffalo with you?" Clara asked.

Durant's face blanched. "Come with me? Are you crazy?"

"No, I'm not crazy," Clara replied, unable to keep the hurt from her voice. "What is to keep me here? If you're going to be up there for an entire month, we could find a place to live, a small house perhaps, and you wouldn't have to stay in a hotel."

"No, it's out of the question."

"But won't you just—"

"I said it's out of the question," the little bank clerk repeated, holding his hand up to stop her from arguing any further.

"I just thought it would be nice," Clara suggested.

Durant forced himself to smile at her. "Yes, but think how much nicer it will be when I come home after being gone for so long," he said. "I have to have something to look forward to that will bring me back. Otherwise, I might decide I want to stay up there."

Clara's eyes opened wide in surprise. Then she smiled when he laughed, intimating he was merely joking.

Brushing away her tears, she asked in a small voice, "Really, Sidney? Will you really be looking foward to coming back home to me?"

"Yes, of course I will be. Now, I must be going. The stagecoach will be leaving soon."

"You'll kiss me good-bye?"

Walking up to the head of the bed, Durant leaned over to give his wife a light peck on the cheek. Abruptly, she grabbed his hand and placed it against her naked breast, holding it fast.

"Good-bye, Clara," he muttered, pulling his hand away and walking quickly from the room. When he was safely in the hallway, he wiped his hand on the leg of his trousers, a look of distaste on his thin mouth. He sighed and then hurried down the stairs and took his overcoat from the peg on the mirrored coat stand at the bottom of the stairs. He put on the coat, checked his appearance in the mirror and then left the house, walking briskly toward the depot, where the money would be delivered to him from the bank.

Across town, in Sheriff Tony Becker's office, Clint Townsend picked up the old blue coffepot from the stove and poured himself a cup of coffee. Like the man he was visiting, Clint also wore a sheriff's badge. He was the sheriff of Johnson County, far to the north, working out of the small town of Buffalo. He had brought three prisoners to Medicine Bow several days earlier, and they were now languishing in the back of the Carbon County–Medicine Bow jail.

Having been a lawman for more than half of his almost fifty-eight years, the tall, solidly built Townsend fit into his profession like a pair of old boots. He had an easy way about him and was usually as unruffled as his slicked-down gray hair, although his clear blue eyes could bore right through a man—especially those on the wrong side of the law.

"Well, Tony, I don't suppose you'll be needing anything else from me," Clint commented and then sipped the strong brew. "I believe I brought all the papers and such regarding those three miscreants, but if you find anything else is needed, let me know, and I'll send it to you."

"Well, it looked to me like you had everything in order, Clint," Tony Becker replied. "But you know these judges. Sometimes they get peculiar ideas and start wanting things nobody's ever heard of before."

"You're telling me," Clint agreed in a dry voice.

He took another sip of his coffee and then grimaced. "What did you brew this with? Axle grease?"

Tony laughed. "I like my coffee strong," he explained. "It helps keep me awake during long nights."

"If you'd hire yourself another deputy, you wouldn't have to work such long hours."

"Yeah, well, you tell that to the Carbon County Board of Commissioners. I'm lucky to have what I got." He grinned, adding, "Fact is, if you want to know the truth, I'm glad your horse went lame and you're having to ride back to Buffalo on the stage."

Clint cocked his head and peered at his fellow lawman through narrowed eyes. "You want to tell me why my misfortune is making you so happy?" he asked.

"Because your misfortune is my good fortune—and it could be yours, too, if we play it right."

"All right, I'm listening."

"Nobody knows it yet, but there's going to be a very large shipment of money—one hundred thousand dollars, so I'm told—being sent up to Buffalo on the stage."

Clint let out a low whistle. "That's a fortune!" he exclaimed.

"Yes, it is. And the bank has offered a bonus to any deputy I can get who will ride up with the shipment. Now, the thing is, a deputy would have to go up there and come back . . . but you're going up anyway. If you was to agree to act as my deputy, I could pay you three-quarters of this bonus and pocket the rest for myself—and I wouldn't have to spare one of my men. I mean, you're going to be on the stage anyway, so what do you say?"

Clint Townsend took another sip of coffee and studied his fellow lawman over the rim of his cup. Tony was correct: He *was* going to be on that stage whether he accepted the deal or not, so if he could pick up a little extra for it, why not? And since he was going anyway, he could afford to take less than a special deputy, thus leaving some left over for the sheriff—and leaving the sheriff with all his deputies.

"All right," he finally said. He laughed and stuck out his hand. "It seems too good an offer to refuse. You've got yourself a deal."

"Good, good. I hoped you would do this. I figure we both stand to gain a little on this, don't you?" Tony Becker paused and then remarked matter-of-factly, "Oh, by the way, I think there are a couple of things I should tell you."

"Okay, what are they?"

"Well, to begin with, I just got word this morning that Zeke Slade and his bunch robbed a bank over in Theresa a few days ago, killing a bank teller and one of the good citizens of the town in the process. That means they are very definitely on the prowl up there— and one hundred thousand dollars might well bring 'em out."

"The money shipment is supposed to be secret, is it not?" Clint asked, perplexed.

"Yes."

"Then if we're lucky, Slade and his bunch won't even know about it."

"True. Oh, but there's one more thing," Tony said. "It's Nate Yeager."

"Nate Yeager? What about him?"

"He escaped from prison a few days ago."

"Did he kill anyone?"

"No." Tony then laughed, explaining, "He put on Bramwell Tyson's duster and hat, stole his horse, and rode out of jail as slick as a fare-thee-well. I tell you one thing, you gotta give that boy credit for gumption, for all that he's a bank robber."

"He's not a bank robber," Clint snapped.

Tony laughed again. "Well, there's a judge and jury that'd disagree with you. They said he is, and that's why he was put in jail."

"I never for one minute believed he was guilty," Clint remarked, his weathered face sobering. He stared into the coffee cup gloomily and then took a last sip.

Sheriff Becker stroked his chin and studied Clint for a long moment and then remarked, "That's right, come to think of it. You were one of those who testified for him, weren't you?"

"Yes."

"But all them eyewitnesses saw him."

"No, they didn't. They saw a bunch of men riding out of town at a full gallop, with their guns blazing. Hell, Tony, you've taken a bunch of townfolk on posses, and you've seen 'em in gunfights. Half of 'em close their eyes when they shoot. You tell me how anyone can make a positive identification of someone who's a hundred yards away, while at the same time trying to dodge bullets."

"Well, what about the marshal?" the lawman asked.

"He's not really a marshal; he's just a town constable. And if you'll pardon my language, he's about as worthless as tits on a chicken."

"You have a way to explain the evidence?"

"It was planted there," Clint said flatly.

"By the marshal?"

"Hell, no. He's too ignorant to come up with anything like that. Besides, just because he's dumb, that doesn't make him dishonest. No, I'd bet my boots that Zeke Slade did it."

"Maybe you're right, Clint," Tony mused after a moment. "But I don't reckon it makes any difference at this point. Whether Nate robbed that bank or not, he's now guilty of breaking out of jail."

"Yeah, I know," Clint said with a sigh. "And if I see him, I'll bring him in."

Zeke Slade was sitting on a boulder near Nate Yeager's dead mount, idly tossing a rock from hand to hand, when the others came back from their search. Standing, the outlaw leader let the rock fall from his fingers and asked, "Find anything?"

"Nary a trace," Slim Hawkins answered. "I don't know who that was last night, but he got away cleaner'n a whistle."

"Yeah, well, he might've got away, but he's gonna have a hard time makin' it outta here on foot," Slade snorted. "Besides which, he ain't even got his canteen with him." Gesturing with his thumb at the gear by his feet, he remarked, "Lookee here. He left it hangin' from the pommel." Lifting the canteen, he added, "I checked over all the other gear and took what I wanted. You boys can have the rest, if you want it." Stowing the gear in his saddlebags, he then remounted.

"Wonder who the guy was," Bill Kelly said, shoving his hat back on his head.

"Probably just some fella wantin' to collect reward money," Slade replied. He laughed, adding, "I reckon he's learned by now that wantin' and collectin' is two different things."

"Slade, you reckon he heard us talkin' about the one hundred thousand dollars?" Slim Hawkins asked.

"I don't know," Slade admitted. "But even if he did, it don't make no never-mind."

"He could maybe warn the folks with the money that we'll be comin' after it," Slim suggested.

Slade laughed, although the laughter never reached his cold dark eyes. "You think that anybody's gonna try and move that much money through here without already knowin' we'd come after it?" He shook his head.

"Anyway, the bank's plannin' on keepin' it secret, so whoever that was nosin' around in the dark last night wouldn't have no idea who to give the warnin' to." Reining his horse around, he commanded, "Come on, boys, let's get a move on. We got some ridin' to do to be in position to pull this job."

"Are we just gonna give up on that fella that was sneakin' around last night?" Luther Murdock wanted to know as they headed out.

"Yep. The son of a bitch'll either starve to death, freeze to death, or die from no water out here. It don't matter which way, he won't be botherin' us no more. You got my word on that."

Nate shielded his eyes and watched the bird. It was the fourth one he had seen alight at a particular spot. If all the birds had been the same kind, he would have presumed that there was a nest there, three-quarters of the way up the side of the rocky cliff. But they had all been different species, and that could only mean one thing: The birds were going to water!

Putting his hands on his hips, Nate studied the sheer rock wall. The place that was drawing the birds was at least two hundred feet above the ground, but though it would be a hard climb, he believed he could do it.

It would be easy, he thought, if he just had a rope. Then he mocked himself, saying aloud, "Yeah, and if wishes were wings, frogs wouldn't bump their asses when they jump." He took a deep breath and then let out a long sigh and started up the side of the cliff.

It was very hard going. When Nate had been at it for roughly a half hour, he looked up toward his destination and groaned. It did not seem that he had gained so much as an inch. However, when he looked back toward the ground, he realized that he was making some progress, for by now he was dangerously high.

Clinging to the side of the mountain, he moved only when he had a secure handhold or foothold—tiny though it might be. Sweat poured into his eyes, and the thirst that had driven him to this state of desperation had been greatly intensified by his efforts. If he was wrong—if the birds were not leading him to water—he had made his situation even worse. He was so desperate for water now that he could feel his tongue swelling in his mouth.

Abruptly Nate came to what appeared to be an impasse. He had progressed four-fifths of the way around a very large outcropping, but now he was stopped because he was unable to find another foothold. Clinging with hands that were fast becoming painfully swollen, he tried to figure out what to do next.

After five minutes, the young rancher reluctantly decided to start back down to see if he could find another way around the obstacle. Reaching for the handhold he had surrendered a few minutes earlier, he then put his foot down on the small, slate outcropping that had supported his weight on the way up. This time, however, the slate failed, and with a sickening sensation in his stomach, Nate felt himself falling. He threw himself against the side, and the jagged rocks scraped and tore at his flesh as he slid downward.

He flailed against the wall with his hands, and after a drop of some fifteen feet, his bloodied hands found the trunk of a juniper tree growing out of the cliff. Grabbing the tree, which, thankfully, supported his weight, he hung suspended in midair. His heart was pounding furiously as he looked down between his feet at the rocky ground some one hundred and fifty feet below. The piece of the slate outcropping that had broken under his weight was still in free fall. Moments later he saw a puff of dust as it smashed against the ground, and then he heard the sound as it broke apart upon impact.

Suddenly his body shifted downward, and he felt the tree giving way. Cold sweat broke out on his brow and his palms. Frantic, Nate examined the cliff face and saw that about four feet away to his right was a narrow shelf. If he could gain that shelf, he would be all right. He took a deep breath and then swung his feet to the right and up—and missed. He felt his body fall another inch as the juniper's roots pulled out a bit more. *Dear God*, he prayed, *don't let me die like this! Not without clearing Cole's and my names!*

Straining with all his might, he swung his leg up again, but again he narrowly missed. He tried several more times, and each time the increased weight on the juniper tree pulled the roots farther out. Nate rested momentarily, listening to his pulse pounding in his ears. Then he tried again, and this time he caught the ledge with the heel of his boot. Breathing another silent prayer, he then slowly worked himself up, away from the juniper tree, until his knees were also on the ledge. Finally, he let go of the tree and pushed up slowly against the rock face until—and at last—he was safely on the ledge.

He sat there unmoving for a few minutes, gasping for air and letting his heartbeat slow to normal. Then, when he had caught his wind and was ready to move on, he looked around and got a pleasant surprise. Rising up from the ledge was a "chimney," a narrow chute that shot straight up the side of the cliff. This natural shaft was studded with rocks in such a way as to almost form a ladder, and within a minute after starting up, Nate recovered the distance he had lost in the fall. The nauseating fear that had overtaken him earlier was now gone, and he climbed easily, finding footholds and handholds so conveniently located that it was almost as if they had been placed there for just such a purpose.

Finally Nate reached the spot where he had seen the birds alight, and he managed to leave the chimney and climb over to a large, flat rock. Just above the rock was a shallow cave, and there, trapped in a cool, shaded reservoir at the bottom of that cave, was a pool of water. With a happy shout, Nate dunked his head into the water and drank deeply.

The engineer blew two long whistles, the signal that he was releasing the brakes, and the train began rolling forward, steam gushing out of the drive cylinders on each side of the engine. Dozens of good-byes were exchanged between those people who remained behind on the station platform and those who were on board, shouting through the open windows.

"Well, there it goes," Nell said, relief in her voice. She sighed. "It seemed like we were on that thing forever." Then she laughed and gestured across the platform, adding, "Though I guess by tomorrow morning, I'll wish we were back on it instead of that."

"That" was a Concord stagecoach. Tough and sturdy from its seasoned white ash spokes to its oxhide boot, it had no springs but was suspended on layers of leather strips, called thoroughbraces—making for a rough ride. The body of the coach was green, and the lettering on the doors was yellow, although the paint was tired and the colors faded, because the coach was at least ten years old and had seen a great deal of use during its lifetime. Still, it was well maintained, as evidenced by the neat and very skillful patchwork done to a few places on the coach body and the leather seats that had sustained some damage during its service. The coach belonged to the Wyoming Express Company, a stage line that connected outlying settlements throughout Wyoming with the railroads that passed through the territory.

Six horses were already in harness, and they stood quietly, awaiting the orders that would set them to their labors, drawing the coach north over the plains and mountains of Wyoming. A baggage cart, laden with the passengers' luggage, was pushed from the train over to the stage. Employees of the depot then began loading the bags onto the coach. They were able to put most of the pieces in the boot, though two large trunks, one belonging to Shannon and one belonging to Nell, had to be lashed down on top.

The two women, one looking elated and the other glum, headed across the platform to the stagecoach. Audible sighs were heard from each as this last segment of their return home was about to begin.

Chapter Three

As Shannon McBride sat on the bench outside the depot, listening with half an ear to Tad Gentry chatter on, she recalled that day in May two years before when she had left home. She had gone out to watch the sun come up one more time over her father's ranch, and even now she could remember how it looked as it climbed higher into the clear blue sky above the Rattlesnake Mountains. Looking down on the sweeping grandeur of the valley, its timbered foothills covered with blue pine and splashed with the rainbow colors of wild spring blooms, Shannon had thought then that her father's ranch was the most beautiful place in the world. She had been sure that neither Boston nor anyplace else the East might have to offer could possibly match it.

Rising before dawn, dressing in denim trousers and a plaid shirt, Shannon had ridden along the familiar ridgeline, picking her way up a trail that led to a secret precipice she had discovered as a little girl and to which she often came when troubled or when she wanted to be alone. From the height of the rocky precipice, Shannon could see the entire fifteen thousand acres of the finest rangeland in Wyoming Territory that made up the Rocking M Ranch, including the main house where she lived alone with her father, the bunkhouses where the forty ranch hands slept, and the barns, cookhouse, equipment shed, smokehouse, and assorted other buildings.

But the young brunette had gone up there to think, not to enjoy the beautiful view. Her betrothed was dead, and her father, thinking she could best recover from her grief in a new environment, had made arrangements to send her East to resume the schooling she had interrupted a few years earlier.

"It will be good for you to see some of the rest of the world," he had told her. "You should know that there are more places to be enjoyed than Buffalo, Banner, Ten Sleep, and Medicine Bow."

Shannon had agreed to her father's recommendation. It was not so much that she was particularly anxious to see new places as it was that she felt she must leave this old place of pain and sorrow. For what her father did not know—and in fact what no one knew—was that while Shannon did feel grief for her fiancé, she felt an even greater grief for the young man she really loved.

She had been able to attend the funeral of the one who died, and there she was comforted by friends. There, too, she had made her secret peace with the departed, begging his forgiveness for the guilt of her deception. But for the loss of her true love she had to grieve in secret, and she could not reveal to anyone that he was the one she really loved, not even to him. To have done so would have exposed her shame at the lie she had been living, and as circumstances had made it impossible to do anything about her true feelings, to have acknowledged them would only have intensified her pain.

As she sat on a fallen log, just on the verge of tears, she knew that she was closing the pages on that chapter of her life and preparing to go forward to what was yet to come.

In the valley below, a wispy pall of wood smoke had spread its diaphanous haze over the cookhouse, and Shannon watched the cowboys, one at a time or in small groups, saunter to the cookhouse for their morning meal. She had seen her father walk out to the barn and begin hitching up the rig that was to take her into town that morning to catch the stagecoach to Medicine Bow, from where she would be able to connect with the train for the East.

She had known, even that morning, that she would be changed by her time in Boston, but she had not foreseen just how much. As she had looked down upon her father's ranch and the only home she had ever known, she had not imagined that there would ever come a time when she would want to say good-bye to this place forever—yet that was exactly her thought as she sat here on the small wooden bench in the Medicine Bow, Wyoming, depot. For one odd moment, she almost wished that she felt differently, but then she recalled the excitement, the vitality, of life in Boston, and she knew she was doing the right thing.

Shannon had made up her mind. There was nothing for her here anymore, and she would not stay in Wyoming. If she could talk her father into going back to Boston with her, all the better. If she was unable to talk him into it, she was determined to go back anyway.

"Well, it looks like they've got the stagecoach all loaded and ready for us," Nell Gentry announced, pulling Shannon out of her reverie. "All we need now is a driver, and we'll be on our last leg home."

"Yes, I guess that's so," Shannon agreed, suddenly feeling trapped in a netherworld between Boston and her father's ranch. She looked over at the coach and saw that the two young men who had been loading the luggage were now walking away. "It's our last leg home."

Across the street from the depot, driver Luke Hightower and his new shotgun messenger, Dingo, were eating dinner at the City Pig Restaurant. Luke was a regular there, and he told anyone who would listen that he considered the City Pig the best eating establishment in the entire territory of Wyoming.

In his early forties, with graying collar-length hair and a very long bushy mustache, Luke had been driving a stagecoach for nearly twenty years. Before that he had driven freight wagons, beginning his lifelong profession at the age of fifteen. Nearly thirty years of sun and wind and heat and cold had weathered his face so that he looked even older than he was. But looking older did not mean he looked frail or infirm, for Luke Hightower was a powerfully built man with wide shoulders, sinewy hands, and arms strong enough to rein a six-horse team with authority, yet skilled enough to impart subtle instructions to each horse through its own "ribbon" when that was needed. He was without a doubt, most agreed, the best driver on the Wyoming Express Company's payroll.

Sitting across from his colleague, assessing him with his light blue eyes, Dingo was a man whose age was more difficult to ascertain—he could have been anywhere from thirty-five to fifty—the determination not made easier by his sparse brown hair. A very short man, just a touch over five feet, Dingo was whipcord tough. Evidence of that toughness was the long scar that started under his right eye, came down over his cheek in an ugly, blue puff of skin and then ended in a fishook, just under the corner of his mouth. Many people had asked Dingo how he had gotten the scar, but he always answered the query with an offhanded shrug. No one had ever had the poor sense to inquire further.

"Luke, would you be wantin' some more 'taters?" Alice Goodberry and her husband, Ben, ran the City Pig Restaurant, and the big-boned woman in her early fifties asked the question with a large, easy smile.

"Don't mind if I do," Luke answered, sliding his plate over to her as she raked a new batch of fried potatoes from a black cast-iron skillet. "Nobody fries 'em as well as you, Alice."

The woman laughed. "Don't you be tellin' Nonnie that," she quipped. "I wouldn't want your wife thinkin' you don't like her cookin'."

"Oh, Nonnie knows I like her cookin' all right," Luke responded. "Fact is, the way I enjoy eatin', why, I reckon I would be kinda hard pressed to find somebody's cookin' I *don't* like."

"What about you, Mister Dingo? You want anything else?" Alice asked the shotgunner.

"Wouldn't mind a few more beans," he answered, not meeting her gaze, and then he picked up a porkchop bone and started gnawing on it.

"You know, Dingo," Luke pointed out, "we're gonna have to take the run all the way to Buffalo without any relief drivers. We was supposed to change at the Powder River Station, but Jason's wife is over at Antelope Springs gettin' ready to foal, and he ain't gonna leave her."

"That's all right. It don't bother me none," Dingo said, shrugging. "If you wanna know the truth," he continued, "I'd just as soon go on to Buffalo as spend any time at Powder River, anyhow. There ain't a damn thing a fella can do at Powder River while he's waitin' for the next trip but sleep and swat flies."

"And smell the stink of oil," Luke added.

Nodding in agreement, the shotgunner remarked, "Which ain't good for nothin' but gettin' it all over you and makin' horses an' cows die from drinkin' the water."

Luke shook his head. "I can't help but feel sorry for all them poor beggars who homesteaded around there, then found that all their watering holes were polluted with that stuff. What good is that land to them?"

Alice came back from the kitchen carrying a pot of beans, and she spooned some onto Dingo's plate. "You boys be careful during this trip," she instructed. "You're gonna have a lot of money ridin' with you."

"A lot of money? What do you mean?" Luke asked, perplexed.

Pointing with her ladle through the front window, Alice asked, "You see that little feller there? The squinty-eyed, hollow-chested little man who's walking toward the stagecoach?"

Luke focused on the man and laughed out loud at the accuracy of Alice's description. He *was* a squinty-eyed, hollow-chested little man. "Yes, I see him."

"That's Sidney Durant," Alice explained. "He's the head clerk over at the bank, and he's married to Clara Montgomery—which means he's working for his father-in-law." She then proceeded to explain about the loans to the northern ranchers, concluding, "Durant's taking the money up there personally—a hundred thousand dollars, from what I was told." She suddenly looked around, making sure no one was listening, and then concluded in a conspiratorial voice, "Only that's all supposed to be a secret."

"If it's a secret, how did you find out?" the driver asked.

Alice bent over the table and said quietly, "Well, Mr. Montgomery and that Durant fella have their lunch in here sometimes, and I overheard them talking. That's how come I know."

"Well, I'm glad to hear of it," Luke remarked. "There was lots of fine folks hurt by the bad winter, and I know they'll be glad to see that some money's comin' in to tide 'em over."

"That may be, but if you ask me, the bank here sure picked out a weasel to handle all the dealings for them," Alice muttered. "'Course, as I said, Sidney Durant *is* Mr. Montgomery's son-in-law, so I reckon he was the one had to be picked, being as he's family. But you tell them nice folks up there around Buffalo to be very careful whenever they're dealing with him. Don't go signing over the family ranch."

Luke laughed. "Alice, it sounds to me like you don't think too highly of Mr. Durant."

"Let's just say that when he married Clara Montgomery, he came out a lot better on the deal than Clara did—and I'm not just talking about the money."

Ben Goodberry came out of the kitchen, wiping his hands on the apron that swathed his ample belly. Coming over to Luke Hightower's table, he laughed softly and put his hand affectionately on Alice's arm. "Is she bendin' your ear, Luke? Woman, come on now. Luke ain't got no time to be listenin' to all your palaver. He's got a stagecoach to drive."

"I was just telling him about—"

"I'm sure I know what you was just tellin' him about," Ben interrupted. "Now, go on. Them muffins you started bakin' need you back in the kitchen."

"All right, all right," Alice rejoined, sighing. She started to walk away from the table when she turned and smiled at Luke. "You be sure and tell Nonnie I said hello, won't you?"

"I surely will," the driver promised.

"And you, Mister Dingo, you come again next time you're in Medicine Bow."

"Yes, ma'am, I'll do that," Dingo promised, still not looking up from his plate.

Ben Goodberry watched his wife walk back to the kitchen and then shook his head, apologizing, "I'm sorry about all her gabbin', Luke. But you know how women love to chatter."

"Oh, I didn't mind at all," Luke insisted. Keeping his voice low, he continued, "Fact is, that was real good information she give me about Durant, 'cause if somebody is plannin' on carryin' a lot of money with 'em on board my stagecoach, why, I'd sure like to know somethin' about it. If we're goin' to be waylaid, I damn well want to know what it is we're bein' waylaid for." He then stood and took a couple of coins from his pocket. "Here's for the supper for me an' my shotgun," he said. "And I'll be needin' a receipt if you don't mind."

"I don't mind at all. Was everything all right?"

"Real good." He looked at Dingo and smiled. "And from the looks of that spankin' clean plate, I don't reckon Dingo had any complaints either."

"It was real good," Dingo agreed, standing as well. "Say, Luke, I almost forgot somethin' I'm supposed to take care of before we head out. I'll meet you over at the stage in plenty of time."

"Okay. Just don't make me have to wait none. The passengers get mighty upset if we ain't ready to go when we're supposed to."

"I'll be there," Dingo promised. Nodding to the restaurant owner, the shotgunner turned to leave. He pushed through the front door of the café, and despite his size—or maybe because of it—he had a swagger about him as he hurried out on his short, bandy legs.

"That's sure a little feller there," Ben noted. "But judging from that scar decoratin' his face, I got me an idea that he ain't someone you'd be wantin' to get on your bad side."

"You've got that right," Luke said.

"I don't believe I've seen him before. Has he been with you long?"

"No, he just started workin' with the company," Luke explained. "Truth is, I don't really know too much about him—includin' his actual name. Dingo's all I know. . . and I don't know if that's his first name, his last name, or even if it's a real name. It might just be what he's chosen to be called."

"Where'd he come from?"

"Don't know that either," Luke admitted, rubbing his chin thoughtfully.

Ben laughed. "You don't seem to know much about him at all."

"Well, I do know he's been around a bit. He's tended bar, worked as a hostler, deputied some, and been a cowboy. Dingo don't talk much when we're rollin', but he don't miss a thing on the trail. And·when you get right down to it, what do you need to know about a shotgun guard anyway? All I really need from him is that he shows up on time, stays sober, and keeps his eyes open. And he does all that just fine."

"We know he's got a good appetite, too," Ben observed, chuckling. He then tore a piece of paper from a writing tablet, jotted down a figure, and signed it. "Here's your receipt," he said, handing the paper over to Luke.

"Thanks," the driver said, sticking it in his pocket. "The home office is real particular about this. Time was when I could just tell 'em what I spent for my meals, and they wouldn't say nothin'. But some folks along the line was beginnin' to take advantage of it. And besides that, prices is gettin' so high nowadays. I mean, who'd have ever thought it'd cost a fella twenty-five cents just to eat a meal?"

Smiling at the restaurant owner, Luke put on his hat and promised, "I'll be seein' you on my next trip down. It don't matter what it costs, it's still the best food in the whole of Wyoming Territory."

"I'm glad you think so. And stay out of trouble," Ben called, as Luke left the café.

As the driver walked across the street, he saw that the luggage was already loaded—which meant he would not have to handle it. "Good," he murmured to himself. "I'm gettin' too old to haul them trunks up top."

The passengers who would be taking the trip were standing on the platform near the stagecoach, waiting for the driver and shotgun guard to show up. The small bank clerk, Sidney Durant, was holding a black satchel to his chest, and he paced back and forth nervously. Luke figured Durant had to be carrying the money in the case from the way he was clutching it possessively. Laughing to himself, the driver thought that the banker was so small that anybody who wanted it could probably jerk the bag away from him, no matter how tightly he held onto it.

Durant approached Luke Hightower as he neared the stagecoach. "It's about time you arrived," he remarked petulantly. "Come on, let's go. We can't wait around here all day."

Luke pulled the watch from his pocket and looked at it. "Take it easy, Mr. Durant. We have eight minutes yet."

"You know my name?" Durant said.

"You was pointed out to me."

"Then no doubt you also know that I am a person of no small importance in this town. And I'm not used to waiting."

"We ain't goin' nowhere till my shotgun messenger gets here."

"Well, where is he?"

"He went to do an errand."

The bank clerk was about to say something else when a woman's voice called out, "Hello, Luke."

Turning, Luke was surprised to see that one of his passengers was Nell Gentry. He smiled broadly and walked over to her. "Nell! Well, now, if you ain't a sight for sore eyes!" he declared. "Do I assume that you're going to Buffalo?"

"I sure am. On your coach."

"Well, now, that's really fine news," Luke said, hooking his thumbs in his belt loops as he studied the beautiful redhead. His voice was filled with delight as he added, "Nonnie's gonna be real happy to see you again. You always was just real special to her. How long are you goin' to be visitin' with us?"

"I'm not visiting," Nell explained. "I'm moving back home. I didn't like Philadelphia, so I'm going to reopen the hotel and live in Buffalo."

"You don't say! Why, look here, that's wonderful!" Luke then smiled down at Tad and ruffled the boy's red hair. "And I'll tell you somebody else that's gonna be right happy to hear this," he told the boy. "Tad, would you believe that since you left last year, Billy hasn't been able to find himself another best friend?"

"I can be his best friend again," Tad declared, smiling.

"Why, I know Billy'll be all for that."

Shannon McBride then stepped forward and said, "Hello, Mr. Hightower."

"Ah, Shannon, girl, you are even more beautiful now than you was when you left us!" Luke exclaimed. "City life sure seems to have agreed with you. Your pa told me you was gonna be on this train. He's really been lookin' forward to your comin' back."

"Yes, well, we'll see how he feels about it when I tell him what I have to say," Shannon responded, sighing. "You see, the truth is that city life agrees with me a lot more than life out here. I'm going to stay only as long as it takes to convince my father to sell the ranch and move East."

"Well, now, why in heaven's name would you want to do a thing like that?" Luke asked, surprised by her suggestion.

"Because, unlike everyone in this godforsaken place, people back East live like human beings."

"Oh, I see," Luke said. He stroked his long mustache as he studied her. "Well, I'm just real sorry you feel that way, Shannon. And as far as you talkin' your pa into leavin' us out here, well, I'm afraid I can't wish you much success in that. All us folks around Buffalo regard your pa with a lot of affection, and I don't think there's anybody who'd care to see him just pack up and move away."

Suddenly Sidney Durant positioned himself in front of Luke Hightower and, ignoring Shannon McBride, pointed across the street, asking, "Driver, is that your shotgun messenger coming out of the Western Union office there?"

"Yes, it is," Luke said.

"Then there's no reason for any further delay, is there?" Durant fumed.

"No reason at all," Luke answered easily, a patronizing smirk on his face. Addressing the passengers, he suggested, "All right, folks, if you're all ready, climb on board, and we'll get started."

While the driver stood watching, the two women and the boy boarded first and then Sidney Durant began to climb inside. Dingo reached the stagecoach just as Clint Townsend passed Luke. The driver greeted his shotgunner, and then he nodded at the lawman, saying softly, "Sheriff, I'm glad you're riding with us. It turns out that one of our passengers is carrying a lot of money this trip, so it'll be good to have extra protection."

Clint stopped in his tracks and stared at Luke Hightower. "How did you know about the money?" the lawman asked, clearly taken aback. "It was supposed to be kept secret."

"Hell, Sheriff, it's our business to know," Dingo replied, answering for Luke.

Trey Farnsworth, who was standing just in front of the sheriff, looked back over his shoulder and added, "Judging from the way the little gentleman is gripping that black bag, I'd say there's a vast sum inside." He pointed to Durant's satchel.

The lawman gaped at Trey. "And *you* even know *who* it is! How in blazes has everyone found out about this? Is there a big sign on the side of the coach?" Clint asked sarcastically.

Trey laid his finger alongside his nose and smiled. "Let's just say it's a matter of professionalism," he replied. "I'm a gambler, you see, and money is my stock in trade. I can smell it."

The gambler and the lawman got into the coach. Trey, Durant, and the sheriff settled down in the rear-facing seat, while Nell, Shannon, and Tad sat in the forward-facing one. The boy was between the two women, lying with his head in his mother's lap and his feet in Shannon's lap, and the expression on his face bespoke his discomfort.

However, when Trey Farnsworth settled into his seat, the look on the boy's face changed to amazement. "Mister," he asked quietly, "can you really smell money?"

Trey laughed heartily. "Well, maybe I overstated

my talent just a bit. I wouldn't actually want to be put to the test."

"You mean you *can't* smell money?" Tad asked, his disappointment evident.

Chuckling, the gambler admitted, "I'm afraid not."

Tad frowned. "Then why did you say you could?"

"Tad!" Nell Gentry scolded, unable to keep the laugh out of her voice. Putting a finger to her son's lips, she told him, "Hush now. It's just an expression, that's all."

The child looked first at his mother and then at Trey. "Oh," he murmured.

"Folks," Luke Hightower announced as he held his hand on the door, ready to close it, "I hope you kept out somethin' warm to wear at night. It's mild enough in the daytime, this bein' May and all, but come dark, you're gonna think you're in the dead of winter. There's still ice in the cricks at night."

Murmurs of assurance rose from the passengers, and then Luke closed and latched the door and climbed up to the box. Dingo was already on top, sitting at his place on the seat with a rifle cradled across his lap. Settling in beside him, the driver released the brake and then took the whip from its holder and popped it over the team's heads. The coach immediately started forward, and within minutes they had rolled down the main street of Medicine Bow and reached the outskirts of town, traveling a little faster than what would be a man's brisk walk.

As the stagecoach rolled north, Trey Farnsworth leaned his head back against the seat. He closed his eyes and listened as Shannon McBride began telling Nell Gentry a story about an adventure she had experienced while in Boston. Soon the gambler dozed off, and he found himself dreaming a dream he had had many times before. Coincidentally the dream concerned a young woman about the same age as Shannon, and it took place in Boston. Trey was able to anticipate with great trepidation the terrible sequence of events as they unfolded, although he was forced each time to relive the images as if he were viewing them for the first time.

The dream would always start the same way. He was in a room near the Boston harbor, and he could hear a bell in a buoy clanging, its syncopated ringing sounding a repeated warning. The traffic outside was muted by the fog, and even the clip-clopping of horses' hooves on the cobblestones was barely audible. Inside the brightly lit room was a young woman who was clearly frightened, but Trey was telling her that she had absolutely nothing to fear.

"I make you a solemn promise that everything will be just fine, Deborah," he reassured the beautiful brunette in his dream. "I give you my guarantee."

"And if it isn't all right?" the young woman always replied, a note of irony in her voice. "How will I be able to call in the guarantee?"

Suddenly the images shifted in time and space, and at this point in the dream, Trey would be shivering and sweating at the same time, finding himself looking down at a woman's bloody, lifeless body. His hands would be covered with the woman's blood as he held them up in front of him and cried out in agony, "No . . . no! My God, what have I done?"

"Mr. Farnsworth? Mr. Farnsworth, are you all right?" a woman's voice called, wrenching Trey from his troubled sleep.

Opening his eyes, the gambler sat up with a start, realizing that he was a passenger in a stagecoach two thousand miles from Boston. His cold, shivering hands were raised in front of him, and the other passengers were all staring at him. The women had expressions of concern and compassion on their faces, while the men and the boy looked surprised and dismayed.

"Mr. Farnsworth?" Nell Gentry asked. "Are you all right?"

Recognizing hers as the voice that had spoken to him moments before, Trey forced himself to smile. "I apologize to you, Mrs. Gentry—indeed, to all of you. I'm fine. It was merely a bad dream."

"You're sure you are all right?" she pressed.

"Yes, quite," Trey murmured. "I thank you for your concern, but really, I'm all right."

Leaning back against the seat, he stared out the window, trying as hard as he could to blot out the painful memory.

Chapter Four

There were no streetlamps in the little hamlet of Soda Lake, Wyoming. It was much too small for such civilized amenities. The lights the stagecoach passengers had seen from a distance as they switchbacked down the mountain road had come from the handful of buildings: a hotel and restaurant, a general store, a saloon, and a livery stable that also served as the stage station. In addition to the five commercial buildings, there were perhaps a dozen houses.

The coach clattered into town, the light from its twin kerosene sidelights illuminating the dusty street. Finally it drew to a stop in front of the livery stable, and the lantern hanging on the sign to illuminate it also dimly lit the inside of the coach.

"Tad, wake up, honey, we're going to spend the night here," Nell Gentry murmured.

Tad sat up and rubbed his eyes. "Where are we, Mama?" he asked, his voice slurred with sleep.

"We're in Soda Creek," Nell answered. Pointing through the window, she explained, "We're going to go across the street and get a room in that hotel over there."

"Nell, I can go on ahead and get our rooms," Shannon offered.

"Thank you. I'd appreciate it," Nell responded. Then she looked down at her son, asking, "Are you hungry, Tad? What would you like for supper?"

"I don't feel like eating," Tad groaned. "My stomach is hurting real bad."

"Still? Oh, dear. I hoped it would have quit by now."

Trey Farnsworth stepped out of the coach first, helped Shannon down and then reached for Tad. He swung the boy down, and Tad winced as he was put on the ground.

"I'm sorry, son," Trey told the boy kindly. "I surely didn't mean to hurt you."

"That's all right," the boy assured him. "I think it just hurts now because I'm tired from sleeping." Looking at his mother, he asked, "Mama, do I have to go to bed right away?"

"Tired from sleeping, huh?" Nell repeated with a laugh. "Well, I'm glad to hear that. You can't be feeling too poorly if you're wanting to stay up."

Luke Hightower and Dingo climbed down from the top of the coach and stretched while a couple of hostlers hurried out to unharness the team and lead them off for food and water. Sidney Durant then stepped out and immediately crossed the street. He was followed out of the coach by Clint Townsend, who stood with the others. The men watched Durant walk quickly toward the hotel, hurrying along behind Tad and Nell.

"Look at how tight that little feller is holdin' that bag. Wouldn't you hate to try and grab it away from him?" Luke asked with a chuckle. "He'd just give you the fight of your life."

The others laughed with him.

"Well, I for one hope nobody tries to take it away

from him," the lawman remarked. "I'm getting paid extra to watch over him, and I'd like nothing better than for the trip to be peaceable."

From the saloon across the way came a woman's high-pitched shriek, followed by the laughter of a dozen or more men. After that a piano began playing, and the notes spilled through the batwing doors into the street. One cowboy came out of the saloon and started up the boardwalk away from the coach, while two other cowboys seemed to materialize out of the darkness in front of the saloon, pushing their way through the doors to go inside. The North Star Saloon was the most brightly lit building in town, and it seemed to draw the cowboys to its glow with the same magnetism with which the gleaming kerosene lanterns here and there were drawing fluttering moths.

"Luke, do you stay in the hotel when you spend the night in this town?" Clint asked.

"No," the driver answered. He stretched and yawned and then scratched his head, ruffling his dark hair. "The company keeps a room for me and my shotgun guard in the back of the livery. Tell the truth, though, it ain't all that invitin', and sometimes I just slide the seats together in the coach and stay in there. It makes up into a fine bed if there ain't no more'n two or three tryin' to use it."

"You planning on doing that tonight?" the lawman queried.

"No, not if you're wantin' to save a little money by usin' it," Luke offered generously.

"Well, I appreciate that. Maybe I will just sleep in the coach."

"Sheriff, if you don't mind some company, I'll stay in the coach with you," Trey declared. He looked over toward the North Star Saloon, adding, "I'd rather spend my money on drink than sleep anytime."

Clint laughed. "Can't say as I blame you. I could use a little snort myself. What say we mosey on over there and have one or two?"

Shannon McBride had managed to get adjoining rooms for herself and the Gentrys. Stopping first in the hotel dining room for supper, the three travelers then went upstairs to their rooms on the second floor.

With the door between the rooms standing ajar, Shannon washed her face and hands at the basin on the table in her room, while in the next room Nell was sitting on the edge of the bed, looking after Tad. After barely touching his meal, the boy was complaining that his stomach was hurting more than ever.

"You know, Shannon," Nell called, "I'm really beginning to be worried about him. It isn't at all like him to be sick like this, and if it had simply been train sickness or something he ate earlier, I should think it would be over by now."

Putting down the towel, Shannon rebuttoned the several buttons she had opened on the neck of her red plaid wool dress and walked into the adjoining room. She leaned over the boy, feeling his face and then remarked softly to Nell, "I'd say he has a slight fever. Tell you what. I'll go downstairs and ask the hotel clerk if there's a doctor in town, and if there is, I'll send for him and then come right back."

"Oh, would you? I'd be very grateful," Nell breathed, her face pale with worry.

Shannon hurried down the stairs and then across the red-carpeted lobby to the front desk. The middle-aged clerk was reading a newspaper by the lamp on his desk, and he lay the paper aside and began preening his thick dark mustache as the beautiful young woman approached.

"Well, now, little lady," the clerk murmured, "what is it I can do for you?"

"Is there a doctor in this town?"

"Well, there's Doc Crader," the clerk said. "Some folks don't think too highly of him, but if you'd like, I could run him down for you."

"Thank you, but the doctor isn't for me," Shannon explained. "I want him for my friend's little boy, who's having terrible stomach pains."

"The little boy, huh? Well, I reckon whatever ails the boy won't tax Doc's skills none. I'll go get hold of him and send him on up to the boy's room."

"Thank you," Shannon replied. "The room number is—"

"We're not that full, miss," the clerk interjected, smiling easily. "You're in two-oh-four, and the boy and his mama are in two-oh-two. Is that right?"

"Yes. How long do you think before the doctor will get here?"

"Very soon, I would think. He's probably just over at the saloon."

"Thank you very much for your kindness," Shannon said, giving the clerk a sweet smile.

Shannon started back up the stairs, and as she did so, Sidney Durant was coming down. Durant put his hand up, stopping her progress. He then took a long, slow, appraising look at Shannon, examining her from head to toe with such unabashed intensity that it almost made her feel as if he were undressing her.

"I was wondering if, uh, perhaps, we might have a drink together?" he asked.

His question surprised Shannon. "A drink? I'm afraid not. Thank you for asking, but I don't imbibe."

"I see," Durant mumbled. "Well," he went on, putting his hand on her forearm, "I want you to know that if there is anything I can do for you, you'll find me just a few rooms down from your own." His hand began moving up and down, caressing her arm.

"Thank you," Shannon responded coolly, pulling away resolutely. "I'm sure I'll be able to handle everything just fine."

She turned, about to continue on up the stairs, but Durant continued talking. "I listened with pleasure to your stories about Boston," the clerk said. "It must be a wonderful place."

"Yes, I liked it."

"I'm sure a young woman such as yourself could have a very pleasant time in a city like Boston."

"Yes, I suppose so," Shannon replied. She did not like the conversation, and she did not like the salacious gleam in the clerk's eyes.

"And if a young woman . . . say a very beautiful young woman such as yourself . . . were to play her cards right with a man with a very bright future . . . say, someone like me . . . then she might find the city even more enjoyable, don't you agree?"

He put his hand back on her arm and began caressing it again.

"A woman like me with a man like you?" Shannon snapped. "That could never be, Mr. Durant."

Durant's face grew dark, and the fingers of his gently caressing hand suddenly clamped down on her arm. "And what is wrong with a man like me?" he asked, his voice threatening. "Are you saying that I am not good enough for you?"

"No, Mr. Durant. I am saying you are married," Shannon replied easily. "And now would you please let go of my arm? You are hurting me."

Durant seemed astonished by his behavior and released his grip instantly. "Yes, yes, of course. Please, forgive me," he muttered. He smiled. "You are right of course. I am married, and that's why I meant noth-

ing . . . improper . . . by my question. I was just suggesting
that the time may come when you may need a friend,
and I am offering myself in that capacity."

"Thank you, Mr. Durant. I shall keep that in
mind," Shannon told him coldly. "And now, if you will
excuse me, I really must go see what I can do for Mrs.
Gentry." Without giving him time to respond, she
turned and hurried up the stairs.

A few minutes after Shannon had returned to
Nell's room, a knock sounded on the door and the
young woman opened it. A short, fat, rather disreputable-
looking man stood there, and Shannon's face fell. She
had been expecting the physician.

"You asked for a doctor?" the man asked.

"Yes," Shannon replied, sighing. "Couldn't he come?"

"Madam," the man countered, pulling himself up
indignantly, "I am he."

The doctor had obviously been drinking, and though
he did not appear to be drunk, he smelled strongly of
alcohol. Shannon had to take a step back to catch her
breath—and to avoid his.

"Where is the child?" he asked.

"He's here, Doctor," Nell called from farther back
in the room. She was sitting on the edge of the bed,
holding a damp facecloth to Tad's forehead. "There's
something terribly wrong with him. I think it's far more
than a simple stomachache."

"Are you a doctor, madam?" he asked, somewhat
churlishly.

"What? No, of course not."

"Then kindly leave the diagnosis to me," Dr. Crader
sniffed, moving over to the bed.

Shannon watched him warily. In addition to being
short and fat, his skin was red and blotchy, and while in
compliance to convention he was wearing business
clothes—a long, dark coat, lighter pants, a vest, and a

string tie—his clothes were extremely unkempt. In fact he had such an altogether unhealthy appearance that Shannon thought her first impression of his being a messenger from the saloon who normally swept floors and emptied spittoons was unfair to floor sweepers and spittoon emptiers.

The physician set his bag down on the dresser, opened it and then took out a flat stick. Putting the stick on Tad's tongue he ordered brusquely, "Say 'ah.'"

"Ahhh," Tad responded.

As the doctor examined him, he pushed the tongue depressor so far down into the child's throat that Tad gagged and then began crying.

"Young man, it's hard to look you over if you're gonna be such a crybaby," the physician mocked.

"Doctor, please," Nell complained, "he's only eight years old, and he isn't feeling well. And frankly, you aren't being very gentle with that stick."

"Madam, if you don't like the way I'm doctorin', you can get another one," Crader rejoined. He put the stick back in his bag, and Shannon wondered if that meant he planned to use it with another patient at some time in the future.

"Is there another doctor in this town?" Nell asked coolly.

"Not for fifty miles, ladies. Not for fifty miles," Crader replied.

"Then we obviously can't get another one, can we?"

"Nope."

The doctor took a look at each of Tad's eyes and then measured his pulse. Shannon glanced at Nell, and when their eyes met, they exchanged a look that said Crader seemed to be acting professionally enough. Finally he completed his examination and stood up.

"Well, you can put your mind to rest, madam," he

said to Nell. "Your boy doesn't have anything seriously wrong with him."

"Thank God," Nell responded, sighing.

"In fact, he's not suffering from any of the usual maladies that I can see. Perhaps the travel has made him somewhat irregular. That would give him a stomachache, sure as shootin'. I'll prepare a purgative for him. That'll clean him out well enough, and he shouldn't have any more problems. It'll cost you twenty-five cents. Do you want it?"

"Yes, of course, if that's what it takes to get him well," Nell replied.

Dr. Crader looked across the room at the water pitcher. "Any water left in that jug over there, girl?" he asked Shannon.

"Yes."

Crader took a small, brown bottle from his bag and handed it to her. "Fill this bottle to about here," he said, indicating with his finger where he wanted it.

Shannon did as directed and then handed the bottle back. The physician riffled through his medical bag and finally extracted an envelope. Opening it, he poured some white powder into the bottle, stoppered the bottle, gave it a good shake, and then handed it over to Nell.

"You go ahead and give him a good dose of it now, and then give him another just before he goes to sleep . . . and keep on giving it to him until he quits complainin'." Picking up his bag, the doctor said, "That'll be a dollar for my services."

Nell walked to the dresser for her reticule, reaching into it and extracting several coins. Handing them to the physician, she told him, "I really appreciate your coming over to the hotel to see him at this time of night, Doctor. And I am very glad that he isn't suffering from anything serious."

"Nothin' serious at all, madam," he assured her. Nodding to each of the women, he then left the room on slightly unsteady feet.

Over at the North Star Saloon, the piano player was grinding out "Little Joe the Wrangler." One of the bar girls was leaning on the back of the piano, singing along off-key, but she was the only one who was paying attention to the music. At all the other tables and along the bar, the cowboys and assorted other patrons were engaged in so many loud, animated conversations that the piano and singer were barely audible.

Clint and Trey had a table near the door. The lawman took a swallow of his beer and studied the gambler over the rim of his glass. "You're the fellow the sheriff back in Medicine Bow told me they were running out of town, aren't you?"

"Yes," Trey acknowledged, nodding, a rueful expression on his face.

"And so now you're coming to my town."

"That's my plan," the gambler admitted, grinning.

"Do you cheat at cards, Mr. Farnsworth?" the lawman asked bluntly, his clear blue eyes staring intently at his companion.

"No," Trey replied. "Did your friend the sheriff accuse me of cheating?"

"Not exactly," Clint responded. He licked the beer foam from his upper lip and then continued, "Tony Becker told me you were so good that you win damn near all the time, but he said that no one had ever been able to actually catch you cheating."

"That's because I don't."

"Then would you mind explaining how the hell you manage to win so often?"

"Sheriff, have you ever heard the expression, 'in the world of the blind, a one-eyed man is king'?"

"Yes, I have," Clint acknowledged, shifting his sturdy body in the chair to lean back.

"You are looking at living proof of that adage," Trey said. "Most men who play poker play it with their heart, with their temper—and with their pride." Touching the side of his head with his finger, he explained, "I play poker with my brain. Since I'm usually the only thinking man at the table, I'm generally the winner."

Clint laughed. "Well, I don't suppose a person could argue with that."

"An awful lot have," Trey rejoined with a snicker. "There's not a town along the Union Pacific that would welcome me back."

"I didn't figure Medicine Bow was the first town you'd ever been run out of," the lawman observed wryly. Leaning forward again, he took another swallow of his beer, finishing it, and then wiped the back of his hand aross his mouth. "But I'll make you this promise. If you aren't cheating, you won't be run out of my town. Buffalo always has room for honest men."

"Well, I appreciate that, Sheriff," Trey replied. "I really do."

Suddenly there was a loud burst of laughter from the bar, and the travelers looked over toward the source. A short, fat man with a red face and big nose, who had come in a few minutes before, seemed to be the center of attention, and he was speaking in a very animated manner.

"Doc, you was in here tryin' to borrow the cost of another drink not more'n a half hour ago," somebody shouted. "And now you got a whole dollar to spend. How'd you come by it?"

"I did a bit of doctorin' on that kid that come in on the stage tonight," Crader answered. He put the dollar on the bar and watched attentively as the bartender filled a large glass with whiskey. Lifting the glass to his

nose, he inhaled the aroma and then sighed with satisfaction just before he tossed the drink down.

"Ah," he breathed after a moment. "That was good,
sir." He snickered, adding, "A damn sight tastier than
that purgative I administered to the kid, I'd wager."
Wordlessly, he held his glass out for more whiskey.

"What was wrong with the kid?" the bartender, a
burly man in his thirties, asked.

The doctor laughed. "Aw, he was complaining of a
stomachache. But if you ask me, he's just a whiner
who's been mollycoddled by his overprotective mother.
There's nothin' wrong with him that a swift kick in the
seat of the pants wouldn't cure."

Those around the doctor exploded in laughter as
the doctor held out his glass yet again and then tossed
down a third whiskey as quickly as he had the first two.

Overhearing the conversation, Trey Farnsworth
turned away in disgust and stared into his beer with an
angry expression on his face. "Somebody needs to take
that gentleman out to the barn and teach him a few
manners," he grumbled.

Clint nodded. "I know what you mean," he replied. "When you share a long trip like this, the
passengers sort of begin to belong to one another, like
cowboys working on the same spread. If an outsider
says something about one of us, it's like they're talking
about all of us."

"That's true," Trey replied. "But it's much more
than that. That man is a doctor—or at least he's supposed to be one. He should show more compassion for
his patient. The cardinal rule of a doctor is 'first, do no
harm.' For that man to administer a purgative without
knowing what was wrong with Tad Gentry is practically
criminal behavior."

Suddenly the town doctor shouted, "Yep, I'd sure
as hell like to be that little brat and have that good-

looking woman caring for *me*! Matter of fact, I think there's nothing wrong with the kid—it's the widow-woman who's ailin'! And what's ailin' her could be healed right quick—if you catch my meanin'!"

The physician's cronies roared with laughter.

Crader continued, "Yeah, that there's one good-lookin' redhead. And I'm thinkin' that maybe I've got just the curative prescription for her!" He grinned salaciously and then shouted, "Me!"

Trey Farnsworth slammed his glass on the table and started to rise, his dark eyes flashing. Clint Townsend grabbed his forearm, but the gambler shook off the restraining hand, saying, "I think this so-called doctor is the one who needs curing... of ill-mannered, boorish behavior."

"Are you sure you want to start with him?" the lawman asked, keeping his voice low. "He's got a lot of friends—and they all may well back him up."

"That's a chance I'm willing to take," Trey muttered. His handsome face stiff with anger, he strode to the doctor's table and stood over him, glaring at him but saying nothing.

Crader finally looked up with watery eyes and asked in a besotted voice, "Something I can do for you, mister?"

"Yes," Trey replied coldly. "You can stop impugning Mrs. Gentry."

"Mrs.?..." The physician's face was puzzled. "Oh! You mean the luscious redhead!" He snickered. "Why? Is she a friend of yours? A *good* friend?"

Trey abruptly reached down and grabbed the doctor's shirtfront, lifting him out of his chair. "She is a mere acquaintance—and a very respectable one. I will thank you to say no more about her or about her son, who is quite ill, although a man of your lack of skill apparently cannot discern it. How you can call yourself a doctor is beyond me. You're a disgrace to the profession!" So saying, he released the man, flinging him down into his chair so hard that Crader's teeth clacked together.

Several of the doctor's friends started to get out of their chairs, but stopped immediately at the sound of a pistol being cocked. Trey glanced over his shoulder and saw Clint Townsend standing there, his Colt .45 trained on one of Crader's friends.

"If any of you try anything, you'll have me to answer to," the lawman snarled. Pulling his jacket aside, he revealed his sheriff's badge, adding, "And as you can see, I've got the authority to use this weapon."

The men looked from the sheriff's face to his revolver to the badge on his shirt and then back up at his face. No one made a move.

Then suddenly Crader stood up, so abruptly that his chair fell over, and he threw a punch at Trey Farnsworth. But the drunken physician's aim was off, and all he got was air. Trey shook his head in disgust and started to walk away, but Crader went after him. Grabbing the gambler's shoulder, he spun him around and then landed a solid right on Trey's jaw.

"You should have left well enough alone," the man in black growled. He then hauled back his fist and slammed the doctor hard on the chin. Crader's feet went out from under him, and he landed on the floor with a thud. He started to rise, but then his head lolled for a moment before he lay prostrate, unconscious.

Flexing his fingers, making sure nothing was broken, Trey regarded his opponent sprawled on the sawdust-covered floor with his mouth hanging open. He was unsure whether the doctor had been felled by the punch or from drink—but then he did not much care. Satisfied with the outcome of the encounter, he nodded to Clint Townsend, who gave a warning glance at Crader's friends and then accompanied the gambler out of the saloon.

Back in the hotel, Shannon McBride and Nell Gentry were discussing the journey. They were speaking softly, for Tad had finally fallen into a restless sleep on the bed behind them.

"I sure will be glad when we get home," Nell said. "Maybe a few days' rest is all Tad needs. It seems as if we've been traveling forever."

"Doesn't it, though?" Shannon said, shaking her head in disbelief.

Nell laughed. "And yet, it's only been a few days since Tad and I stepped onto the train in Philadelphia. When I think of all the people who made this long journey before the railroad was built—why, it makes me positively ashamed for feeling sorry for myself."

Shannon mused, "My mother and father came West on a wagon train." She sniffed, adding, "They could hardly wait to get out here . . . and I can hardly wait to go back."

Nell smiled. "Oh, now, Shannon, I wouldn't be so quick to decide that, if I were you. Perhaps you'll surprise yourself and come to feel that this is where you belong after all. Surely there are some things about it that you remember fondly."

"Oh, yes," Shannon admitted. "Seeing that sunrise this morning reminded me of all the sunrises and sunsets I used to enjoy on my father's ranch. And I remember the way the bighorn sheep would play on the mountainsides and the sounds of their hooves clattering against the rocks when they would break into a run." A faraway look came into her eyes, and she continued, "I always loved hearing the cattle late in the evening, when the cows would start calling out to their calves. And I confess that I miss being able to ride a horse . . . I don't mean ride a horse sidesaddle in a city park while wearing some stylish riding habit. I mean really ride like the wind, dressed in a man's denim trousers and shirt." The young woman's eyes sparkled brightly as she talked.

"See, what did I tell you?" Nell enthused, her auburn hair catching the light as she nodded vigorously. "You're going to find that you missed it out here more than you thought."

"No, I don't think so," Shannon responded, playing distractedly with the tassel on her nightgown. She was quiet for a moment, and then she said softly, "I do miss all those things, that's true—in fact, I miss them terribly. But I'm afraid there's nothing here for me anymore."

Nell reached across the table and put her hand lightly on Shannon's. "Dear, I know what you are feeling," she murmured. "I went through the same thing when my darling husband died. All I wanted to do was escape that place where we had lived together, escape it and the memories. But life does go on, after all, and I've learned now that there's more sweetness to the memories than there is pain. And who knows? Perhaps there'll be another man in my life someday." She smiled brightly. "If so, I wouldn't want that man to be a Philadelphia dandy." Giggling, she concluded, "I saw enough of those gentleman this year to last a lifetime."

Shannon laughed. "How about a Wyoming dandy?" she asked, her eyes twinkling mischievously. "Someone like Mr. Farnsworth, perhaps?"

"Shannon!" Nell gasped.

"Now, don't tell me you haven't noticed him," Shannon teased.

Blushing, Nell looked down at her hands for a moment. Then she looked up and smiled broadly. "Well, perhaps I did notice a little. But I think you're wrong when you call him a dandy." A frown suddenly creased her forehead, and she commented, "You know, there's something about him that bothers me."

"Troubles you?" Shannon asked.

"No, I wouldn't exactly say that it troubles me." She sighed and then observed, "During all those years my husband and I ran the hotel in Buffalo, I saw more than my share of professional gamblers. I got to the point where I could pick one out the moment he came through the front door, no matter how he was dressed. Now, I'm sure Mr. Farnsworth is indeed a professional gambler as he says, but I'm also sure that there is more to that man than meets the eye." She paused and then added, "And I have to admit that he is quite a handsome man."

Shannon countered, "Yes. Well, I suppose he is handsome. Not as handsome as Mr. Durant, of course, but he is handsome."

"Not as handsome as Mr. Durant?" Nell blurted. Then, because Shannon had told Nell about the incident on the staircase, she realized that the young woman was teasing. She began laughing so hard that tears came. Finally she managed to get control of herself long enough to wipe the tears from her eyes and titter, "Oh, yes, Mr. Durant is quite handsome—but, alas, we mustn't forget, as you reminded him, he *is* married."

"Oh, such is the pity," Shannon managed to remark wryly before dissolving in laughter with Nell.

Finally, their laughter having subsided, the two women hugged each other affectionately and bid one another good night.

"We've got a long day ahead of us," Nell commented. She glanced over at her son. "I certainly hope that purgative will have helped Tad. The journey is uncomfortable enough, without feeling sick."

Patting her friend's shoulder just before she returned to her own room, Shannon assured her, "He'll no doubt be just fine. You'll see."

Chapter Five

Using his hat, Nate Yeager fanned the sparks until the kindling caught. He was cold and he was hungry, but now he was finally about to relieve both conditions.

Within a couple of minutes the fire was burning, and he started tossing more twigs onto it until it was a fairly respectable blaze. That done, he tended to the rabbit he had managed to kill a short time earlier, by the first light of dawn. The rabbit would be the first food he had eaten in two days, and he had been lucky to get it, for he had shot it with his very last bullet. Skinning it by using a sharp piece of shale, Nate then spitted it on a green twig and hung it over the flame.

A short while later, sitting with his back against the wall of the cave after devouring the last of his rabbit, Nate found himself thinking about his brother and about the future they had tried to build together. He and Cole had come West with their mother after the war, when both were very young children.

It had been a decision of necessity for his mother, for with her husband dead and two small boys to raise, Ruby Yeager had to support her family, and she did so by teaching school. Though she had been a schoolteacher in Missouri before the war, the educational requirements to teach there had changed, and Ruby was no longer qualified. Then she read a newspaper article noting that the western states and territories were so desperate for teachers that their educational requirements were not as strict. On the strength of that article, Ruby moved her family to Colorado and taught for many years.

For as long as Nate could remember, he and Cole had wanted to own their own ranch, and when they were grown, they left home to pursue their ambition. There were several stops along the way in the early years. Nate had been a hired hand for other ranchers, he had driven a freight wagon and worked as a shotgun guard, and he had driven a stage. Finally, a couple of years earlier, he and Cole had managed to get a ranch started, and while it had been rough going in the beginning, they stayed with it.

It had always been their intention to bring their mother to Wyoming to live with them once they had the ranch established. That notion was brutally destroyed when, on the very dawn of their success, Cole had been killed and Nate sent to prison.

All the time he was in prison, Nate had received letters from his mother as regular as clockwork, for Ruby never seemed to lose hope, and each letter would tell of some new plan she had for getting him released or some person she had contacted on his behalf. Then one day Nate got a letter from one of the lawyers she had been working with who informed him, with regret, that his mother had succumbed to a fever.

The sudden and unexpected death of his mother had hit Nate as hard as anything that had happened to him since he had been sent to prison. But ironically her death had led to his freedom, for Nate would never have tried to escape if his mother had still been alive.

Now Nate hoped his freedom would not end up being short-lived as a result of the decision he had reluctantly come to. Having at one point driven the stagecoach between Medicine Bow and Buffalo, he knew that it would be coming through this part of the country later that morning. He also knew that if he was going to survive, he had to meet that stage. The danger lay in the chance that he would be recognized, and if the people on the stage were aware that he was an escaped prisoner, he would have no choice but to give himself up. Even if he had had ammunition, he would not put up a fight. That would mean injuring or killing innocent people—and that was something Nate Yeager would never do.

It was barely light when the coach pulled out of Soda Lake, and all the passengers had reclaimed the same seats they had occupied the day before. By now they had learned the skill of getting comfortable in a close and rough-riding coach, and they leaned their heads back, propped their feet against the seats opposite to minimize the jostling, and then quickly dropped off to sleep.

Trey Farnsworth dreamed again, and again his sleep was troubled by disquieting visions from his past.

"Are you sure you want to go through with this?" a man in a surgical gown asked. "The malignancy has progressed much too far—and as you well know, such a procedure has never been tried before."

"Not in America, but it has been successfully demonstrated by Andral in Paris," Trey replied, looking down at the operating table. He then lowered the sheet that had been covering the face of the anesthetized patient—and it was the same beautiful young woman to whom he had given his guarantee that the operation would be successful.

The assisting surgeon shook his head. "Dr. Farnsworth, I have the utmost respect for your surgical skills—but removing a malignant tumor is extremely difficult, and removing it from the abdomen is nearly impossible. She may well die on the table."

Trey looked over at the assisting surgeon and replied levelly, "I gave her my word that she will come out of it successfully."

Shaking his head again, the assisting surgeon declared, "I pray that you won't live to regret a promise made in desperation."

Trey ignored the comment and picked up his scalpel to begin the delicate operation. All went well until he was about to close the abdomen, then suddenly the woman began to hemorrhage. Although the young doctor worked frantically to stop the bleeding, the woman's blood pressure dropped precipitously, and despite Trey's best efforts, she died on the table.

Barely hearing the other surgeon telling him that it was not his fault—that she would have died anyway, even had he not performed the risky operation—Trey Farnsworth looked down at her lifeless body. He then stared at his hands, covered with her blood. The hands that had been so successful in dozens and dozens of operations had failed him now, when he needed them most.

Holding his hands up in front of him, he cried out in agony, "My God, what have I done? Her blood truly is on my hands. If I had not been so eager to try the new procedure, if I had not been so arrogant as to think I could do what dozens of other surgeons have not, she would still be alive. Then it would have been up to God, not me, whether she lived or died."

"You mustn't do this to yourself, Dr. Farnsworth,"

his colleague insisted. "You let yourself get too close to the patient."

"I was going to marry her, Doctor," Trey retorted coldly. "She was my fiancée. How much closer could I get?" He looked down at the table and then picked up the lifeless hand of the young woman. "I'm sorry, Deborah," he whispered in a choked voice, kissing the hand tenderly and then releasing it.

Turning his back on the operating table, he dropped his scalpel on the floor and walked away, determined never to pick up a surgical instrument again. He hurried out of the operating theater and closed the door firmly behind him, firmly closing the door on medicine as well.

Trey awakened with a start, and it took a few moments for him to realize where he was: riding the stagecoach to Buffalo, Wyoming, not walking the halls of Boston Mercy Hospital.

Dr. Preston Gordon Farnsworth had left the hospital and removed all his funds from the bank, and then he had gone to the railroad depot that very day, altering his name and taking the first train going west. Within weeks he had become a professional gambler, using his skilled hands to manipulate decks of cards rather than surgical tools and plying the saloons and gaming houses all over the West.

For the nearly ten years he had been out West, he had not communicated with anyone from his past. He had not sent so much as one word to any of his friends or colleagues back in Boston telling them he was alive or where he was or what he was doing.

Once, about a year ago, he was surprised to read an article about himself in a newspaper in Denver. "Whereabouts of noted surgeon still unknown," the headline had read. The story related how, after losing his betrothed on the operating table years before, Preston Farnsworth, M.D., had disappeared. According to the article, some people believed he had gone to Europe to practice medicine, while others believed they had spotted him on Boston's skid row. One person swore Trey had become a ship's surgeon, sailing the big windjammers to China. No one had guessed where he really was—or what he was doing.

The others in the coach all stirred awake as well, and as the gambler looked out at the eastern sky, he estimated that the sun had been up for nearly three hours. Just then he felt the coach begin to slow, and he glanced ahead and saw a man standing in the road, waving his arms to flag the stagecoach down.

On top of the coach, Dingo raised his shotgun, but Luke put out his hand to stop him. "Hold it," the driver ordered. "I recognize that young fella. That there is Nate Yeager. He's a friend of mine. Matter of fact, he used to drive for this company." Luke immediately hauled back on the reins and set the brake on the coach, bringing it to a halt.

Down on the road, Nate smiled broadly in recognition. "Hello, Luke," the escaped convict called. "It's good to see you."

"Well, Nate, I didn't know you was out of prison," Luke replied, grinning as well.

"I received a pardon," Nate lied.

"So what the hell are you doing out here on foot?" Luke asked. "Seems like a pretty foolish place to be."

"You're right. It is," Nate agreed, laughing. Running a hand through his sandy hair, he grinned sheepishly and explained, "Like a damned fool, I lost my horse and gear the other night. I've been wandering around ever since. Could you give me a lift?"

"I'd be glad to," Luke said. "I've got a full load, though. You'll have to ride on top."

"Suits me fine. The ride's better up there anyway," Nate quipped. He started toward the side of the coach when the door was suddenly opened, and Clint Townsend stepped out, his gun drawn.

"Hello, Nate," the lawman said, his experienced eyes assessing the young convict. "I heard about you breaking out of the penitentiary. I guess you know I'm gonna have to take you prisoner."

Nate sighed and then smiled. "Well, Clint, I reckon it's better than dying out here in the cold," he countered. He looked up at Luke. "Sorry about the lie, Luke. Clint's right. The truth is I escaped from prison about a week ago."

As the sheriff stepped in front of Nate and removed the revolver from his holster, the prisoner told him that it was empty. Clint then placed handcuffs on the young man's wrists.

Sidney Durant had been leaning out the window, watching what was happening, and he angrily leapt down from the coach, clutching the black satchel tightly to his chest. "Now, wait a minute! Just hold on here, Sheriff! You don't intend to bring that outlaw along with us, do you?" he blustered. "Especially in view of what we're carrying on this stage."

Nate squinted at Durant and then asked, "That little black bag you're carrying there. It wouldn't happen to contain about one hundred thousand dollars, would it?"

Clint Townsend looked at his prisoner completely askance. "What the hell—? Nate Yeager, how do you know about that?"

Nate grinned ruefully. "Well, the truth is I didn't just lose my horse, I had him shot from under me. You see, I broke out of prison hoping I could capture Zeke

Slade and force him to prove my innocence. I stumbled on his camp the other night and was sneaking around, trying to figure out how I could capture him, when I heard him telling his men that they'd soon have one hundred thousand dollars to divvy up. That's when I happened to kick loose a piece of shale and they got on to me. They chased me out of there and killed my animal, but I managed to get away in the dark—and here I am." He grinned, adding, "Slade wasn't none too specific about where the money was going to come from, but when this man started popping off, why I just put two and two together."

"Well, you came out with four all right," Clint confessed. "But what I'm wondering now is how did Slade find out about it?"

"I don't know, but if it's on this stage, he must be lying in wait up ahead," Nate suggested. Then he grinned again. "I guess that means I'm going to get another chance at him after all."

"Sheriff, I refuse to be a passenger or to allow the money I am carrying to be on the same stage with an escaped convict," Durant grumbled.

"Well, I'm not leaving this man out here, Mr. Durant," Clint replied, his voice impatient. "For one thing, it wouldn't be Christian. And for another, he's a wanted man and I'm a sheriff. I have to do my duty. So you've got no choice—unless *you* want to get out here and walk the rest of the way."

"It's a disgrace, an absolute disgrace," the bank clerk muttered. "If anything happens, I shall hold you personally responsible. That's a promise!"

Nate Yeager was about to climb up to the box when Clint motioned him toward the passenger compartment. "Nate, you'll ride inside where I can watch you better. There's no room on the seats, but you can ride on the floor."

Shrugging, Nate remarked, "Well, I'm not going to enjoy it as much, but I'll oblige you." So saying, he stepped inside, giving everyone a casual, sweeping glance. "Hello, folks, hope you don't mind the intru—" he stopped in midsentence at the sight of Shannon McBride. "Shannon," he gasped. "What...what are *you* doing here? I didn't think I'd ever see you again. I heard you had gone back East, to finish school."

"Hello, Mr. Yeager," Shannon replied coolly.

"'Mr. Yeager'?" the young rancher retorted. "It was never Mr. Yeager before."

Shannon frowned at the handcuffs on Nate's wrists. "You were never a bank robber before," she countered.

"I'm not a bank robber now," he insisted.

"The court says you are."

"The court said the same thing about my brother," Nate said softly. "But I heard you were at his funeral, nevertheless."

"I could hardly do otherwise," the young woman rejoined. "After all, Cole and I were engaged to be married."

"And tell me, Shannon, when you were standing there beside my brother's grave, did you really believe he had robbed a bank?"

Shannon closed her eyes tightly, and tears trickled down her cheeks. She wiped them away quickly, almost angrily, and then turned and stared out the window.

When a moment or two had passed without her giving Nate an answer, he realized that none was coming.

On top of the coach, the driver whistled and shouted to his team. With a resounding crack of the whip, the stagecoach got under way again. "Answer me, girl," Nate almost shouted above the clacking wheels. "Did you really believe my brother robbed that bank?"

Shannon turned and faced him. "No," she answered quietly.

"Then you can't believe that of me either. We were set up by Zeke Slade."

"I know that's the story you told at your trial," the young woman murmured.

"It was the truth, every word of it."

"Then why—" Shannon began, but her voice broke slightly. Taking a deep breath, she went on, "Why didn't the jury believe you?"

"Maybe I can answer that question," Clint Townsend suggested. "I was at the trial, you may remember."

Smiling at the lawman, Nate told him, "I've never forgotten how you gave testimony on behalf of my brother and me. And I'm still grateful for your try."

"Yeah, well, I wish I could've done more. But to answer your question, Miss McBride, the reason the jury didn't believe him was because in a way it wasn't Nate Yeager who was on trial, it was the entire community of Banner."

Nell Gentry looked at the lawman curiously. "What do you mean by that, Sheriff?" she asked.

"Well, when Zeke Slade and his boys held up that bank, the whole town turned out to defend it," Clint explained. "But you may recall that Slade got away and one of the townspeople got killed. That made them even more determined to run Slade down and get revenge. So when they found Nate and Cole, why, they figured they had redeemed themselves somewhat. Now, don't forget that the jury was made up of citizens from that same town, and they weren't about to deny the community its success. I don't think they intended to sentence an innocent man, I think they just refused to accept defeat—and if Nate had been proven innocent, in their eyes it would have been a defeat."

Nell looked down at Nate and told him kindly,

"Well, I'd known you ever since you and Cole moved to the area and started your ranch, and if it means anything to you, I always thought you and your brother were innocent."

"Thank you, Mrs. Gentry. It does indeed mean something to me."

"This is a lot of poppycock!" Sidney Durant fumed. "Sheriff, would you listen to yourself and the others? You're saying the only reason Yeager was found guilty was because he was tried in Banner. But if the people here are any indication, he would have been found innocent just by virtue of being tried in Buffalo! So nothing has been proven. The real test would be to try him somewhere other than Banner or Buffalo."

"That's just what I hoped to do by breaking out of prison," Nate remarked wryly. "I wanted to capture Zeke Slade and then force another trial in a neutral location. I would be quite willing to accept the decision of that jury."

"Well, I am not from Banner or Buffalo, and were I to serve on such a jury, I would find you guilty," the little clerk proclaimed.

"Without hearing the evidence?" Nate asked.

"Seeing you here in handcuffs is evidence enough for me," Durant proclaimed. "You are an escaped criminal, and I intend to regard you as such." Facing the lawman, he added, "And what's more, Sheriff Townsend, I demand you do so as well. After all, you are a public servant, and I am carrying a great deal of money that is desperately needed by people in your own county. How do you think it would look to the ranchers there if the money they needed was lost because of your incompetence?"

Clearly trying to control his temper, the sheriff muttered, "Mr. Durant, why don't you just relax and keep quiet? I'll see to it that the money gets through all right."

Sitting on the floor of the coach with his back against the door and his knees drawn up before him, Nate looked up at Trey Farnsworth and smiled. "I don't believe I've had the pleasure," he announced.

The gambler smiled down at him. "Trey. Trey Farnsworth."

"I'm—"

"Nate Yeager. I know." Trey smiled. "Your reputation precedes you, Mr. Yeager."

"Call me Nate."

"Nate . . ." Tad Gentry piped up, but his mother quickly shushed him.

"Tad, you are not to call an adult by his first name. You are to call him Mr. Yeager."

"But, Mama, he just said to call him Nate."

"He told *Mr. Farnsworth* to call him Nate. Mr. Farnsworth is an adult; you are a child."

Laughing, the prisoner declared, "I don't mind if he calls me Nate. Friends call each other by their first name, after all, and I'd like for Tad to be my friend. If it's all right with you, Mrs. Gentry."

"Is it all right, Mama?"

Sighing, Nell conceded, "I suppose."

"Nate, I'm not feeling real good. Have you ever been sick?"

Nate looked from the boy to his mother and then back again. "Well, I sure have, and I'm sorry to hear that you're feeling poorly. But I'm sure you'll be better real soon."

After that, they rode in silence for a while, the passengers lost in their own thoughts. Several times Nate glanced up at Shannon, sensing that she had been watching him from the corner of her eye. But each time he looked up, she glanced away, refusing to acknowledge him.

Nate had been very surprised to find Shannon on this coach. If his life had not taken such an unexpected and tragic twist, Shannon would have been his sister-in-law by now. He had often thought about that while he was in prison—about what it would have been like to have had the beautiful young woman married to his brother.

Would he have been able to remain on the ranch? To be that close to her and yet maintain a cool distance? What would he have done? How would he have lived with the fact that he was in love with his brother's wife?

It was that terrible secret that Nate Yeager carried with him. He had been silently and hopelessly in love with Shannon McBride, his brother's fiancée.

Feeling a pang of guilt each time Nate glanced at her, Shannon looked quickly away. Her heart was beating rapidly, and she hoped he would not notice the effect he had on her. Why did he have to show up now? She had closed the door to her past. She had buried Cole Yeager— literally—and with him, she thought, the terrible dilemma of being engaged to marry one man while being secretly in love with his brother.

She was not prepared to have the door to her past reopened, not even by so much as a crack, and she found herself wrestling with a tumult of emotions. A wild part of her, so deep inside her heart that she had never before realized that it existed, was ready to run away with him now. If he were to ask her, she would gladly forego the wonders of Boston civilization and her own plans to take her father back with her. Willingly, she would run away with Nate Yeager to take whatever life had to offer, as long as they could face it together.

"No!" Shannon cried.

"I beg your pardon, dear?" Nell asked.

Shannon looked over at Nell. Realizing that she had spoken the word aloud, she felt her cheeks flush with her embarrassment, and it was as though her word still hung in the close atmosphere of the coach. She had been fighting so desperately against the wild dictates of her heart that the intensity of her battle had spilled from her lips without her having intended for it to do so.

"Oh," Shannon finally said. "I'm sorry, Nell. I must've dozed off and talked in my sleep. My apologies."

Nell chuckled. "I understand, dear. It's been a tiring trip for all of us." She looked down at her son and brushed his red hair from his freckled face. "Tad's been so good," she said softly to Shannon. "You know, I don't think that doctor did the least bit of good last night." She shook her head. "I might have more confidence if he had been sober."

"Mrs. Gentry, his face appears flushed," Trey Farnsworth suddenly observed. "Does he have a fever?"

Nell felt Tad's face and then nodded. "Yes," she answered. "Yes, he does." Taking the canteen from the floor, she wet her handkerchief and placed it on the boy's forehead. He looked up at her through pain-filled eyes.

Removing his own handkerchief from his pocket, Trey handed it to her. "Wet this one as well, and put it on the back of his neck," he suggested. "It'll help bring the fever down."

"Thank you," Nell replied, smiling at the gambler. She reached into her reticule. "I should probably give him another dose of this purgative—though it hasn't worked so far."

"May I see it?" Trey asked.

"Yes, of course," she replied, handing it to him.

Trey unstoppered the bottle, smelled it and then made a face and shook his head.

"I wouldn't give any more of this to your son if I were you," he advised.

Durant looked over at Trey and snorted in distaste. "I hardly see where a man like you comes off telling the lady not to administer a curative that was prescribed by a doctor," he remarked.

"A drunken doctor," Nell pointed out in a sharp voice.

"But a doctor, nevertheless, madam. This man is nothing but a common gambler."

"That doesn't mean he can't have a gift for doctoring," Clint Townsend put in. "I've known lots of people with such a gift, and if they've got common sense and sober thought to go along with it, I'd say they're worth listening to as much as anybody."

Tad suddenly pleaded, "Mama, I don't want to take any more of that. It tastes horrible!" He had no sooner said the words than he leapt off Nell's lap, pushed his way to the window, and then stuck his head out. He gagged a few times, though nothing came up from his empty stomach. His face even paler than it was, Tad then climbed back onto his mother's lap.

Shaking her head, Nell Gentry declared, "We'll listen to Mr. Farnsworth. You don't have to take any more."

Everyone fell silent again. Despite the discomfort, the rocking motion of the stagecoach lulled the passengers, and all of them—including Nate Yeager—soon fell asleep.

Chapter Six

The stagecoach passengers had become accustomed to the long, tiring, bone-jarring ride, and throughout the rest of the day they dozed frequently. Trey Farnsworth managed to relieve some of the monotony of the waking hours of the journey by demonstrating card tricks for the others, and everyone was impressed by the dexterity of his hands and fingers—with the exception of Sidney Durant. The bank clerk made an obvious show of his total disdain for anything so trivial as card tricks, and he pointedly ignored the display, staring glumly out the window.

When the novelty of the card tricks had worn off, the passengers began exchanging stories. Clint Townsend, who had been a trooper in Custer's cavalry, told of the bloody massacre at the Little Bighorn. The lawman explained that he had been with Reno's troops, and he was therefore spared the fate that befell Custer and his men.

Nell Gentry listened attentively and then added a little bit of information that the sheriff had omitted. "He's much too modest a man to tell this part of it," she explained, "and I wouldn't have known myself had a visiting Army officer not informed my husband and me one day. You see, Clint was awarded the Medal of Honor for his part in that battle."

"The Medal of Honor!" Trey exclaimed. "Well, Sheriff, I am very impressed."

"All I did was get a little water for some of my comrades," Clint mumbled. "It hardly seemed like something to get the medal for. Still," he added, a faraway look on his face, "it was a proud moment when President Grant pinned it on me."

When it was Nell's turn to entertain the others, she told a story of the night Bat Masterson had stayed at her hotel and then had a gunfight before breakfast the next morning. "It was over so fast that I wasn't even certain I saw it happen," she quipped. "A jump of the shoulder, a loud pop, a cloud of smoke, and a man lay dead in the street while Bat Masterson stood over him, a smoking gun in his hand."

"I remember that," Clint put in. "I was a deputy then."

"Did you attempt to arrest him?" Trey asked.

"There was no reason to. There were more than a dozen witnesses to the incident, including Mrs. Gentry here, and they all swore that the man drew on Masterson without any provocation."

"I was out on the ranch when he came into Buffalo," Shannon McBride recalled. "Papa wouldn't even let me come into town to see him—although I was very curious. What did he look like?"

"Oh, he was quite the handsome peacock," Nell said, chuckling. "He had coal-black hair and slate-blue eyes. But what really made him stand out was the way he dressed." Nell smiled. "He was what you might call a fancy-Dan dresser." She then glanced at Trey Farnsworth, as if suddenly aware of the similarity of clothing. Their eyes met, and he smiled, but she quickly looked away, embarrassed.

Shannon then shared with the others some of the wonders she had encountered in Boston—such things as the telephone, electric lights, elevators, and magic-lantern shows.

"I was reminded of all the mean tricks I've seen our cowboys pull on the dudes from the East," she said, giggling, "for I was a 'rube' from out West and as fair game for their jokes as any tenderfoot ever was for a bit of western fun. Once, when we were painting one of the rooms of the dormitory, the other girls sent me to a store to buy some spotted paint."

The others in the coach laughed.

"I know, I know," Shannon agreed, "it sounds perfectly ridiculous to think I would fall for something like that. But you must remember, my mind had been bedazzled with all the inventions of modern society— inventions we had never even heard of out here, much less seen. I was perfectly willing to believe that there was such a thing as spotted paint."

Nate was next in the line of storytellers, and he soon was regaling everyone with a hilarious story of some of the antics of his fellow prisoners.

When everyone had fallen silent, Shannon asked the gambler, "What about you, Mr. Farnsworth? Do you have a story you could share with us?"

Trey looked thoughtful for a moment and then told about a balloon ascension he had once made in France. "I went aloft with the celebrated aeronaut Gaston Tissandier," he told the others. "It was a most exciting excursion, and I was given the job of monitoring the other passengers for oxygen deprivation, while of course making certain that I didn't get into trouble myself.

"As we got to fourteen thousand feet, we all began to get a little giddy. From there on up, I insisted that we use the oxygen in greater and greater doses. Then disaster struck. The gas-relief valve froze on the balloon, and for a while we were afraid we would keep going up and up without stop. Then suddenly—and fortunately—the balloon burst, and our descent was assured . . . although it was at a far more rapid rate than we would have wished," he concluded wryly.

"How was it you weren't killed?" Nell asked, on the edge of her seat from the excitement and tension of the story.

"When the gas bag exploded, it formed a huge, inverted cup, much like an umbrella," Trey explained. "Consequently, it set us down as gently as a feather."

"My, what a marvelous adventure!" Nell declared, her eyes shining with pleasure, and the others added their own words of appreciation for his story.

"Poppycock!" Durant scoffed. "You might have the others convinced, Farnsworth, but not me. What would a gambler be doing in France?"

"I haven't always been a gambler, Mr. Durant," Trey murmured. "You, on the other hand, have probably always been a jackass."

Trey's rejoinder brought an outburst of laughter from the others in the coach. Sidney Durant merely clutched his black satchel to his chest even more tightly while he fumed in silence.

Shortly after that the coach stopped, and Clint Townsend leaned out the window, a slight breeze ruffling his gray hair. "I wonder why we're stopping here," he asked rhetorically as he pulled his head back inside. "This isn't the way station."

"Sheriff?" Luke Hightower called down from up top on the driver's seat. "Sheriff, you want to come out of the coach for a minute?"

"Sure thing," Clint replied, opening the door and stepping outside. He walked a few steps forward and then looked up at Luke, who was standing on his seat and pointing toward a small cluster of buildings about a quarter of a mile ahead.

"As you know, that there's Powder River Station," the driver said. "We're supposed to change teams and spend the night there—but I don't know. I don't like the looks of it. I don't see no smoke nor nothin'. It just don't appear to be right."

Shading his eyes, the lawman looked ahead. Finally, shaking his head, he suggested, "Well, we aren't going to find out anything by staying here, so you may as well drive on in. But be real careful."

"Hey, Sheriff," Dingo called, his weathered face screwed up with concern, "are you any good with a long gun?"

"I reckon I can hit what I'm aiming at," Clint answered laconically. "Why do you ask?"

"Well, sir, besides this here shotgun I'm carryin', I got two Winchesters up here in the boot. I'd be obliged iffen you'd take one of 'em and come up on top till we get into the station."

Nodding in agreement, Luke added, "Yeah, as a matter of fact, I believe I'd appreciate that myself, if you don't mind."

"All right," Clint answered.

"Sheriff, what's wrong?" Sidney Durant called, sticking his head out the window. "What's going on?"

"Mr. Durant, you and the others just stay put inside," Clint answered. "I'm going to ride on top of the coach until we get into the station."

"What about this escaped criminal we have in here?" Durant asked in a disbelieving, reproving voice. "Are you just going to leave him in the coach with us? We are unarmed and helpless. If he decides to try something, who will protect us from him?"

"Don't be afraid of him, Durant. You've got Tad and the ladies to watch out for you," Clint countered.

The others laughed appreciatively at the remark, which only served to rile the banker more. "See here, Sheriff! This is no laughing matter," Durant said angrily. "I demand you do something about this prisoner."

"Mr. Durant, you certainly are one for making demands," Clint growled. Sighing, he said, "All right. Nate, why don't you climb up on top with me?"

"Suits me," Nate agreed easily. Exiting the coach, he climbed up to the luggage rack and then sat down and leaned back against the trunks. Clint climbed up alongside him and then took one of the rifles from Dingo.

"All right, Luke," the lawman said, "you drive her on in and let's see what we can find out."

Nodding, the driver nudged his shotgunner. "Dingo, you keep your eyes open. If you see anythin', you let me know and I'll snap a whip over these critters so fast, they'll think they're gettin' ready to run that there Kentucky Derby."

A few minutes later the coach pulled into the depot. Halfway between the corral and the main building, a man was lying unmoving on his stomach.

"That there is Marcus Powell," Luke announced softly, pointing to the body as he halted the team. "He's one of the hostlers here."

Just then the door opened on the coach, and Clint Townsend ordered sharply, "Stay inside the coach! All of you!"

Trey Farnsworth called back, "Sheriff, I'd just like to take a closer look at that man over there, if you don't mind. Perhaps he's still alive."

Weighing the idea for a moment, the lawman relented. "All right, I reckon you can take a look if you want to. I'm pretty damn sure there's nothing you're gonna be able to do for him, though."

Stepping out of the coach, Trey walked over to the body. Squatting down behind him, he put his hand on the man's cheeks to test his body temperature. He then moved the hostler's arms and legs to test the degree of rigor mortis.

Turning to the driver, Clint asked Luke, "See anything?" Both the driver and the shotgunner were standing on top of the stage, sweeping the area carefully with their gazes.

"No, I don't see nothin'," Luke replied. "How about you, Dingo?"

"No, I don't see nothin' either. Maybe I'll just climb down and take a look around," he volunteered and then flicked a glance at the lawman. "If that's all right with you, Sheriff."

"Yeah, sure. Go ahead," Clint replied, never taking his eyes from the scene.

Dingo hopped down from the coach and began looking around the station. It was quiet—so quiet that the silence itself became a presence. That was particularly evident when the windmill behind the one-story log building responded to a breeze and suddenly swung around with a loud squeaking clank and then started spinning.

Like the others, Clint was startled by the sudden sound, and he swung his rifle toward the stable, only to see the windmill whirling into life.

Nate Yeager then stepped down from the coach and looked up at the lawman. "Sheriff, have you noticed that there are no horses in the stable?" he mentioned, motioning toward the corral.

"Yeah," Clint answered. "I noticed that."

Dingo had neared the front porch of the main building when he suddenly stopped. He stared for a

moment and then came back to the coach, walking back
at a much quicker pace.

"What is it?" Luke asked. "What did you find?"

"There's two more bodies over there," he said,
pointing. "I think one of 'em might be the stationmas-
ter. Both of 'em's been shot."

Clint rubbed his chin thoughtfully and then asked,
"What do you think, Dingo? Is this the work of Indians?"

"No, I don't think so," the shotgun guard answered,
scratching his sparsely covered head. "Leastwise, whoever done this sure ain't acted like no Indians I've ever
saw. All of 'em was shot, and there's no scalpin' and no
knife wounds."

"Well, whoever it was, I don't think they're around
here anymore," Luke offered. "I mean, it seems too
damn quiet for that."

Trey came back to the stage and looked up at Clint.
"If it means anything, that man over there hasn't been
dead for more than three or four hours," he said.

Nodding, Clint responded, "It probably means
that whoever did this has been gone that long."

"In that case, is it all right to let my passengers
out?" Luke asked. "I hope you ain't plannin' on keepin'
these folks in the coach forever," he went on. "They got
to be able to get out and stretch their legs a bit.
Especially the ladies, if you know what I mean."

"Yeah," Clint said. "I know what you mean. But,
before we let them out, let me check the outhouses,
just to make certain there are no unpleasant surprises
waiting inside. In the meantime, Dingo, you want to
get a tarp or something over those bodies?"

"I'll do better'n that, Sheriff," Dingo offered, starting
back toward the barn. "There's gotta be some shovels
kept back in the barn. I'll get 'em buried."

Clint Townsend watched Dingo's retreating back
for a moment, and then he hopped down and made a

thorough check of the area. Coming back to the stage-coach, he opened the door to the coach, telling the passengers, "Okay, folks, it seems safe enough. You can come on out now, if you want to."

"Thanks," Nell Gentry said, brushing back a stray lock of her auburn hair, which was glistening with sweat. "I don't think I could have stayed in this coach for another minute."

As the passengers wandered around the station, Luke and Dingo dug graves for the three dead men. "We'll leave a letter for the next coach that comes through here, tellin' what we did," Luke explained to Clint. "I don't want to take them poor fellas on the stage with us, but there's no way we can just leave them lyin' out here."

"I agree," the lawman said.

Coming alongside the men, Nell Gentry looked at Luke and asked, "Mr. Hightower, would it be all right if I look around the kitchen? Perhaps I can find something to fix for our supper."

"I think that would be a grand idea, ma'am," Luke answered. "I hadn't thought of it, but now that you mention it, I am mighty hungry."

"Nell, would you like some help?" Shannon McBride offered.

"I'd love some help," Nell replied. The redhead then put her arm protectively around her son's shoulders. "Come along, Tad. You stay inside with us, out of everyone's way."

Sidney Durant was sitting on the boarding step of the coach, an annoyed expression on his face. When Clint Townsend neared, the bank clerk pointed over toward Nate Yeager, who was wandering around the yard, examining the tracks that had been left in the dirt. "Sheriff," the little man asked, "are you just going to let your prisoner roam around free like that?"

"What do you mean, free?" Clint replied. "Can't you see that his hands are manacled?"

"That isn't enough," Durant countered. "He should be chained to a tree or to the wheel of the stage or something. He shouldn't be allowed to roam around like that. For all we know, it might have been him that killed all these people here. You are placing every passenger on this coach in jeopardy."

Sighing impatiently, the lawman stared at his interlocutor. "Durant, you aren't seriously trying to blame these killings on Yeager, are you? How in hell could he have done them? He was with us."

"He wasn't with us last night. He joined us this morning, if you remember," Durant remarked stiffly. "Who is to say he didn't do this during the night and then ride away from the scene of the crime? Perhaps his horse went lame along the way, and that was why he was out on the trail looking for a ride. Or he could even be riding with us to establish his alibi."

"Come on, Durant, you're not making any sense! You heard what Mr. Farnsworth said. These men have been dead no more than three or four hours. That means Nate couldn't have done it."

"Do you mean to say you are going to take a gambler's word on how long these unfortunate victims have been dead?" Durant asked scornfully.

"Why not?" Clint snapped. "His guess seems as good as anyone else's."

"Nevertheless, I am making a note of this," the clerk promised, "along with the several other errors in judgment I have seen you make. And I will hold you accountable for them."

"You just go ahead and do that, Durant," Clint retorted with disgust.

A heavy silence fell, which was broken when Nate

called, "Sheriff, you want to come over here and take a look at this?"

More than willing to oblige, Clint walked over to where Nate was standing.

"Mr. Durant still giving you trouble, is he?" Nate asked dryly, giving the fastidious little man a sidelong glance.

"He's trying to," Clint admitted. "But never mind him. What have you found?"

Raising his manacled hands, Nate pointed to some hoofprints in the dirt. "You see this tie-bar shoe?" he asked. "While I was sneaking around Zeke Slade's camp, I noticed that one of their horses was shod this way." He gestured toward the main building, adding, "This is Zeke Slade's work."

"Zeke Slade, huh?" Clint mused. "Yeah, I was afraid of that. And if they know about the money, that means they're after us. But what gets me is why did they have to kill everyone here?"

"I imagine they wanted to run the horses away so they could keep us from having a fresh team," Nate answered. "That would sure give them an advantage— and the only way they could do that would be to kill the men who work here." Shrugging, he added, "I suppose the only reason they didn't stick around and attack us here is they were afraid some other coaches might come along as well."

"That means they're going to be waiting up ahead, aren't they?" Clint asked.

Nodding, the prisoner replied, "That's my guess. So, what are you going to do?"

"Well, I reckon I'm gonna have to give this a little thought," the lawman answered, shaking his head. Folding his arms across his broad, muscular chest, Clint Townsend stared into the distance, his eyes unfocused, as he considered their dilemma.

By the time the bodies were buried and the horses watered and fed, Shannon came out to announce that supper, which consisted of fried salt pork, biscuits, and gravy, was ready.

"Sorry about the fare, gentlemen, but this is all we could find," Nell Gentry apologized as the men filed inside the station building.

"It smells awfully good to me," Nate remarked, and the others concurred.

As they all sat down around the table, Clint Townsend called for their attention. When everyone quieted down, he told them, "I'd like to talk some things over with you folks. Judging from the tracks that Nate spotted, it's more'n likely that Zeke Slade and his bunch were the ones who murdered the men here, meaning it's likely that they know about the money. And it's possible that they're figuring on hitting us tonight, while we're asleep. I think we should go on—even though there's a damn good chance that they'll be waiting up ahead for us."

Luke swallowed a chunk of biscuit and then pointed out, "The problem with goin' on, though, means we're gonna have to take this same team right back out without a rest after they've been workin' all day."

"I'm afraid that can't be helped," Clint responded. "I think it's too dangerous to stay here . . . especially with the ladies and the boy."

"We could maybe head on over to Antelope Springs and put the ladies off there," the driver suggested.

"No! I'm for going on," Shannon McBride replied. She smiled sheepishly at the forcefulness of her remark and then added, "I mean, I didn't want to leave Boston in the first place, but I did. And now that I've come this far, I don't intend to be put off by the likes of Zeke Slade."

"I agree with Shannon," Nell agreed. She put a plate of food in front of her son, her expression encouraging, but Tad merely looked at it listlessly. "I've come too far to stop now." She laid the back of her hand on her son's freckled face. "Besides, I want to get Tad to Dr. Presnell as quickly as I can."

"I, too, feel we should go on," Sidney Durant agreed.

"Well, there's a switch," Clint remarked dryly, an amused expression on his face. "I was sure you would want us to turn around and go back."

Giving the lawman a look of disdain, the bank clerk said huffily, "I have an obligation to the people who are waiting for this money. Regardless of what you may think of me, Sheriff, I am a banker, and I hold that responsibility very seriously."

Shrugging, the sheriff looked at the gambler. "Mr. Farnsworth, how about you?"

"Whatever the others want is fine with me," Trey said. "I have no preference one way or the other."

"All right, then. We'll push on ahead."

"I have a suggestion, Clint," Nate Yeager offered.

"Let's hear it."

Laying down his fork, the young rancher ran his finger along the right side of it to illustrate his point and suggested, "The regular stage road goes along the east side of these mountains, along the Powder River. Instead of taking it, why don't we go up Willow Creek?" Shifting his manacled hands, he moved his finger along the opposite side of the fork. "That's on the west side. Slade and his gang won't be looking for us there."

"I don't know," Clint replied slowly, rubbing his stubbly chin as he pondered the idea. "I've been that way on horseback a couple of times. Some of that country is mighty rough. And frankly, I don't know if we could get the stage through that way."

"I remember a wagon trail that the miners used to

use," Nate said. "We can take the stage anywhere they could take their wagons."

"It's possible, I suppose," the lawman murmured. Turning to the driver, he asked, "What do you think, Luke?"

"I can't rightly say for sure," Luke answered as he studied Nate's fork over the rim of his cup. "Nate's correct about one thing, though. There is a wagon route that goes up the west side." He paused for a moment and took a sip of his coffee; then he went on, "It'd be hard goin', but I think it could be done."

"There's a problem ain't neither one of you is considerin'," Dingo pointed out, the words somewhat muffled by the food in his mouth.

"What's that?"

"Well, we ain't changin' the team *here*, so that means that if we go up the west side, we ain't gonna be able to change the team for the whole rest of the way. The coach can maybe make it through the trail, but the problem is, can the horses make it? They may get so plumb tuckered out that they just drop, right in their harness."

"Not if we baby them as much as possible," Nate suggested. "We can leave all the luggage here, locked in the storeroom, and send a wagon back for it later. We'll take only a few necessities—including whatever food and cooking utensils we can rustle up here. And when we have a pretty steep grade, all the passengers could help things along by getting out and walking."

"It might work," Luke admitted.

"Wait a minute! Hold on here!" Sidney Durant interjected. "I'm against all this!"

"I thought you were wanting to go on ahead," Clint said, looking at the man through narrowed eyes.

"Yes, I did, as long as we were going to go by the regular route," Durant replied. "But this man is a known outlaw. I mean, what do we know about him? He suddenly appeared on the trail this morning, telling us he was set afoot by Zeke Slade. Well, I don't believe him. I think it's likely that he's in with that gang of thieves and cutthroats, and now he's just trying to set us up for an ambush. If we go on the west side of the mountains, there won't be anyone we can turn to for help."

Clint Townsend stared at the stiff little man. "If Slade and his bunch hit us out there on the trail, there won't be anyone we can turn to for help, no matter *which* side of the mountains we're on," the lawman rejoined. "And if they're looking for us on the east side, then the west side is our best bet."

"Unless, of course, this man has arranged for Slade to be there."

Sighing impatiently, Clint remarked, "I've known Nate for a long time. Like I said before, I believed him at his trial when he said he was set up by Zeke Slade, and I believe him now when he says he overheard them making plans. And I *don't* believe he would try and set the rest of us up for an ambush. He's not the kind of a man that could do something like that." Throwing up his hands, he added, "But the decision isn't mine to make. Luke, you're the driver. What do you say?"

"Well, I tell you, Clint, I've known Nate about as long as you have, and I don't believe he's in with that bunch either. And since Slade is most likely waitin' for us up along the Powder River road somewhere, then I think we should go up Willow Creek."

"Dingo?"

"I'm paid to ride shotgun, Sheriff, not make no decisions," Dingo replied as he broke open two more biscuits and covered them with gravy. "You want to take this here coach to China, well, I reckon I'll be sittin' up there on the box the whole way... long as I get paid."

He shrugged, stating, "Go whichever way you want to. It don't make me no never-mind."

"Sheriff, may I raise a concern?" Trey asked.

"Go ahead."

"You're a lawman, and if you believe Mr. Yeager is telling the truth, then I certainly have no reason to doubt it. But in case you have forgotten, we have a sick boy with us. He needs to get to Buffalo as quickly as possible. Now, which way is faster?"

"The Powder River route is faster by at least half a day, maybe more," Luke replied.

"Then, for the boy's sake, perhaps we should take that route . . . or at least give his mother the option of being the deciding factor."

"Mrs. Gentry," Clint asked. "Do you want us to keep going home this way?"

"No," Nell answered emphatically. "You remember that horrible incident about a year ago, when they found a rancher, his wife, and their little girl and little boy murdered? Everyone knows Zeke Slade is the one who did it. It might mean Tad being sick for a bit longer before he sees the doctor, but I'd rather him be sick than dead." She shuddered slightly, adding, "And if Zeke Slade finds us, I'm afraid that's what we'll all be."

"Then it's decided," Clint announced. "We'll go by way of the Willow Creek wagon road."

"Dingo," Luke said, wiping his mouth with a napkin and getting up from the table. "What say you and me go outside and start unloadin' the stagecoach? We need to get it as light as we can."

"Anybody gonna eat this last biscuit an' piece of meat?" Dingo asked, pointing at the platter. When no one answered, he made a sandwich and then took a bite of it as he quickly followed Luke out the door.

Clint then stood and walked around to Nate. "We

won't be needin' these things anymore," he said, unlocking Nate's handcuffs.

"What?" Sidney Durant sputtered angrily. "Just what do you think you're doing?"

"If Zeke Slade figures out what we're doing and comes after us, we're gonna need every gun we've got," the lawman replied.

"Sheriff! You don't seriously intend to—"

"I certainly do intend," the lawman interjected, cutting Durant off. Drawing himself up to his full, commanding height, he asked sharply, "Does anyone else object?"

"The more guns we have, the safer I'll feel," Nell Gentry agreed.

"You'll certainly get no objections from me," Trey added.

Shannon McBride was watching the young prisoner with admiration. "Nor from me. I trust Nate completely."

Smiling, Nate promised the young woman, "You won't be sorry."

Angrily, Durant stormed out of the building, slamming the door behind him.

"You're going to need this as well," Clint told the young prisoner, handing Nate his revolver.

"With bullets?"

Clint smiled. "Oh, yes. You did tell me it was empty, didn't you?" He shoved a dozen slugs out of his gun belt and handed them over. Nate pushed six of them into empty slots on his own belt and then loaded the other six into the cylinder of his pistol.

"Dingo tells me there's an extra rifle, too," Clint said.

His blue eyes regarding the lawman intently, Nate smiled and replied softly, "Thanks, Clint. I won't betray your trust."

"I know you won't."

Chapter Seven

It had been a long time since the mining road had been used, and the route, though passable, was extremely difficult. At one point, the stage lurched so sharply to the left that everyone inside was thrown against each other or the sides of the stagecoach. Tad Gentry cried out in pain, and Nell comforted him as best she could, although her eyes betrayed her concern.

"We were fools, absolute fools to come this way!" Sidney Durant yelled.

"We all agreed that this was the way we were going to come, Mr. Durant," Shannon McBride pointed out.

"No, we did *not* all agree. I never consented to this decision."

"You got on the coach, Mr. Durant," Clint Townsend reminded the clerk, his clear blue eyes boring into him. "By that action, you agreed."

"Whoa!" Luke Hightower suddenly shouted from his seat on the box, and the coach came to an abrupt halt.

"Now what?" Durant asked.

Nate Yeager, who had been riding on top of the

coach, climbed down and dropped to the ground. Opening the door, he announced, "Folks, I'm afraid you're all going to have to get out and walk a bit. There's a pretty steep grade coming up, and we're going to need to lighten the coach."

Trey Farnsworth stepped out of the coach first. Turning to help the others, he held out his hand to prevent Tad from getting out when the boy appeared in the doorway. "I think it would be best if you stayed in the coach, son," he told him kindly. "You don't weigh enough to make that much difference, and you shouldn't be walking."

"Do you think that would be all right, Nate?" Nell asked, poking her head out the doorway over her son's shoulder.

"Sure," Nate replied. "Trey's right. He doesn't need to walk."

"I can walk," Tad insisted. "I'm not a baby."

"I know you're not a baby, Tad," the young prisoner replied kindly. "That's why I think you could do something for me, if you would."

"What?"

"Well, somebody has to stay inside and keep an eye on things for us in there. Since you weigh the least, I was sort of hoping you would do it. You can even lie down while you're doing it."

"Oh. Sure, all right," Tad agreed. His face was pale, and his eyes were slightly glazed as he moved back into the coach and lay back down.

When Durant got out, he looked up at the driver's seat where Luke sat holding the reins. "Mr. Hightower, just so that you fully understand, I want you to know that I shall be writing a letter to the Wyoming Express Company, demanding a refund of my fare. I paid to *ride* to Buffalo, not walk."

"Yes, sir," Luke replied. "I'm sure you'll be writin'

to the company with all kinds of complaints. From what I can tell, you don't ever seem to run out of 'em."

"And I'll add surliness to my list of complaints as well," Durant promised, shaking his finger angrily. "There's no excuse for you to be discourteous to your passengers."

"I reckon not." His voice amused, Luke said, "Now, if I ask you real polite, would you please walk in back of the coach along with all the other passengers?"

Sniffing derisively, the bank clerk did as he was asked, clutching his satchel protectively to his thin chest.

With everyone walking along behind the coach, the driver whistled to the team, and they started up the grade. It was a long, gradual climb, and the coach moved no faster than the passengers were walking. When they finally reached the top of the hill, Luke gave the horses a few minutes to rest, and then he informed the passengers they could reboard.

It was late enough in the day now that the western sky was ablaze with color. Shannon McBride was watching the sunset through the window on her side of the coach, and she exclaimed to her friend, "Oh, Nell, would you look at that beautiful sky? How could I have ever let the loveliness of these sunsets, the beauty of this wild, rugged country, slip away from me? Boston has much to offer, I'll admit—but it has nothing to compare with all this."

Nell chuckled. "Is this the same Shannon McBride who was on the train with me? The young woman who was so resentful of having been brought back and who could hardly wait to convince her father that the only sensible thing to do was sell his ranch and move to Boston?"

"There have been a few changes in the way I look

at things since then," Shannon admitted, her face flushing slightly.

Nell reached over and squeezed her hand. "I'm glad to hear that," she said. "You and your pa are real good people, Shannon, and if Wyoming ever becomes a state, it's going to be because we have a lot of people like you and your pa out here."

The coach hit another bump at that moment, and Tad made a sharp little cry.

The redhead immediately became solicitous of her son, saying, "Oh, Tad, honey, I wish I could make the hurt go away."

"Mrs. Gentry," Trey said quietly, "perhaps the boy would be more comfortable if you undid the top buttons on his trousers and loosened them. That would take some of the pressure off his stomach."

"Yes," Nell agreed. "Yes, I'm sure that's a good idea. I hadn't thought of that." She started to unbutton Tad's pants, but the boy put his hand down to stop her.

"No, Mama," he complained. "If you do that, when I walk, my pants will fall down, and people will laugh at me."

"Honey, you heard what Nate said. He wants you to stay in the coach and keep an eye on things. You aren't going to have to walk anywhere," Nell reminded him.

"And besides, if anyone happened to laugh at you, I'd put 'em in jail," Clint offered.

"You promise?"

"I promise."

"All right," Tad agreed, nodding solemnly. "You can unbutton them, Mama."

"How does your stomach feel now, Tad?" Trey asked, his concern evident.

"That does make it feel better," Tad told him. "But it still hurts somethin' awful."

Nell smoothed back the boy's red hair and promised, "We'll soon have you at Dr. Presnell's. Then you'll be fine."

Listening to the conversations inside the coach from his seat on the roof, Nate Yeager thought that what he had missed most being in prison were the little things that everyone takes for granted when they have their freedom. He had almost forgotten how pleasurable it was just to have a quiet talk with a good friend—without having a guard watching, thinking you were planning something. How he had missed walking in the woods, feeling the springy softness of pine needles underfoot while listening to the song of some bird. Or the simple pleasure gotten from sitting on a porch swing, moving lazily, while watching a sunset.

Yeah, he thought to himself, *I've forgotten what normalcy feels like as opposed to the artificial existence of being in a cage.*

When the coach had to be emptied again a half hour later, Nate hopped down and walked directly behind the coach. Shannon McBride dawdled about ten yards behind the others, taking in the beauty of the mountains. Nate's heart began to pound as he watched the beautiful young woman, and he dropped back to walk alongside her.

"I can't tell you how good it is to see you again," he told her, keeping her pace.

"Why?" she asked.

"Why? Well, because . . . because you were my brother's fiancée," he told her, shrugging. "And I wanted to make certain that you understood that Cole and I didn't do what they said we did."

"I guess I never believed that you did," Shannon admitted, looking down at her feet.

"You didn't?"

"No."

"But you went away. You left to go to school in Boston."

"Yes, that's true—although actually it was my father's idea, but I went along with it. You have to understand that there was nothing left for me here. I...I couldn't bear to ride by your ranch every day...seeing all the work that you and Cole did and knowing how close the two of you were to your dream— only to see it going to waste. Cole was dead, you were in prison and...and I felt all empty inside."

"I do understand that," Nate murmured.

"Was it...was it awful in prison?"

Nate smiled wryly. "Well, the whole idea of a prison is to make it a place that a person never wants to see again," he explained. "The hope is that after such an unpleasant experience, a man will reform when he gets out rather than do something that will send him back."

"Does it work?"

"I don't think so," Nate answered, sighing. "In fact, I think it just makes most men harder. I'm not saying people like Zeke Slade don't deserve to go to prison—or hang, for that matter—I'm just saying that the experience inside a prison generally makes a man worse than he was when he went in."

"But it didn't make you worse," Shannon offered, touching Nate's arm briefly. "You are as sweet now as you were when you were going to be my brother-in-law."

Nate looked intently at Shannon, searching her face. "You know, that wasn't something I was looking forward to," he confessed.

"You mean you didn't want to be my brother-in-law?"

"No."

"Why not?" she asked lightly. "What are you trying to do, hurt my feelings?"

"No," Nate said softly. "I was trying to keep from hurting Cole."

"I don't understand."

Taking a deep breath, the young prisoner told her, "I'm afraid I never really thought of you as a sister-in-law. I had other, more personal thoughts than that— thoughts that I didn't think I could share with anyone."

"Oh!" Shannon exclaimed, and her face changed abruptly. For a fleeting moment, her face held a look of pure delight. Then, just as quickly, it clouded over, and she shook her head fiercely. "Nate, you really shouldn't—" the young brunette began, but Nate put his hand out to stop her.

"No, wait, let me speak," he insisted. "Cole is dead now, and he has been for two years. I never said anything about this before because it wasn't my place. You were engaged to Cole and I wouldn't do anything to hurt you or him. When I was in prison, I was in no position to even let myself think about such things, let alone say them. But now there's no one left who could be hurt, and there's no reason—"

"No, don't say it!" Shannon begged, interrupting him. "Please, Nate, don't say it!"

Puzzled, he muttered, "You don't know what I'm going to say."

Shannon looked up at him through tear-filled eyes. "Yes, I do know," she half-whispered. "You are going to tell me that you love me."

He stared at her, surprised. "But how could you know? I've never said anything about it before. . . . I've never so much as breathed a word about it."

"Nevertheless, I know," Shannon murmured, looking away. "And the reason I know is that I feel the same way about you." She then gazed at him again, her face beseeching. "But we couldn't speak of it then, Nate, and we can't now. Don't you see? We mustn't."

"Shannon!" Nate blurted, barely hearing her last words. "Did you mean what you just said? Could it be true that you love me?"

"Please, Nate, don't make me say it. I beg of you."

Nate suddenly reached for her, but she broke away from him and ran to the stage. Then she walked quickly around to the opposite side of the coach so that he could not see her, and he knew that she wanted to regain her composure.

The young prisoner was as puzzled by what he felt was her odd behavior as he was elated that she felt about him the way he did about her. It took all his willpower to keep from rushing to her to take her in his arms and kiss her, telling her that everything would be all right. But he knew that at that moment she was like a frightened bird, and the best thing he could do would be not to frighten her more. Reluctantly, he did not pursue her.

When they reached the top of the grade, Luke Hightower let the horses rest again. By now the sun was just below the horizon, and the red of the sunset was turning to purple, while the purple was already turning to black. It would be dark before much longer, and the passengers had already decided that they were not going to try to push through all night. However, Luke did have a particular place in mind where he wanted to make camp, and that was another five miles or so. There, Luke told them, they could find water, and as it was in a little valley, they would be able to have some shelter from the cold night wind.

Dingo was tending to the horses, and seeing him standing alone near the head of the team, Nate walked up to him. He had been looking for the opportunity to speak with the shotgunner alone, and now he looked around to make certain no one was close enough to overhear them.

"Where were you in prison, Dingo?" he asked without preamble.

Surprised, Dingo gasped and looked up at him sharply. "Who told you I was ever in prison?" he demanded.

"You did."

"Me? Why, I never did no such thing! What makes you say I told you?"

"There's a look a person gets when he's inside," Nate explained. "That look never goes away, no matter how long ago it was. You have that look, my friend."

Dingo was quiet for a long moment; then he glanced back at the others. Finally he let out a long sigh. "Yeah," he said. "I reckon I do know about that look. Please don't say nothin' about it, Nate. Nobody else knows, and if the company found out, I'd most likely lose my job. I can't see the Wyoming Express Company hirin' a man who once served time for robbin' a stage. And it's awful hard tryin' to go straight if you ain't got no job."

"I surely do see your point," Nate replied. "When were you in?"

"About five years ago," the bandy-legged guard answered, fingering the scar on his face.

"Here in Wyoming?"

"No. It was back in Kansas."

"Kansas?" the rancher echoed. "Zeke Slade was in the state prison there about five years ago, wasn't he?"

Dingo's eyes narrowed, and he nodded cautiously.

"You met him there, didn't you?" Nate guessed.

Looking at him warily, Dingo replied, "Yeah. Fact is, Zeke Slade was my cellmate."

While the others took the opportunity to leave the wagon road and go into the surrounding woods to refresh themselves, Trey Farnsworth walked over to talk to Nell Gentry, who was looking in through the coach window at her son.

"Are you doing all right?" he asked, gauging her carefully.

"Yes, I'm doing just fine, thank you," Nell answered, smiling at him. She nodded toward the inside of the stage. "I wish I could say the same for Tad, poor thing."

"Is he sleeping now?"

"Yes."

"Well, that's the best thing for him at the moment," Trey advised. "If he's asleep, he's totally relaxed, and the more relaxed he is, the less strain he puts on his stomach muscles—hence the less pain he's going to feel." Sticking his hand in through the open window, he felt Tad's face. "He's still fevered," he said. "Although, for the moment, it doesn't seem to be out of hand."

She cocked her head and stared at him for a long moment, then said, "Clint is right. You really do have a feel for doctoring, don't you?"

"Well, I thought I did... once," the gambler answered without elaboration.

"Maybe you should be a doctor."

Trey smiled at her sadly. "No, I'm afraid I can't agree with you there."

They were both silent for a moment, and then Trey said, "Tell me about this man in Buffalo, your doctor there. I believe you said his name was Dr. Presnell?"

"Yes, Robert Presnell. He's an older man who has experienced just about everything. He's certainly done his share of removing bullets and arrows and repairing broken bones and such. I believe he's a very good doctor, and he's pulled a lot of folks through some pretty bad times."

"Do you have faith in him?"

"Yes." Nell got a distant look in her eyes before

continuing. "He wasn't able to save my husband, but I'm convinced that he did everything he could. Yes, I'd say that I have faith in him."

"Then that's the most important thing," Trey remarked. "And if you want my opinion, I would say that you are very lucky that the doctor back in Soda Lake did nothing for Tad except prescribe a purgative."

"A useless purgative."

An acrimonious look came over the gambler's face. "If it was just useless, that wouldn't be so bad. In Tad's case, the doctor's purgative may even have been harmful. I strongly recommend that you throw the bottle away."

"I already did," Nell admitted.

Trey smiled. "That's good."

"You've been most kind to look after Tad as you have, Mr. Farnsworth. And I would like to thank you."

"Please, we have shared so much of this journey now. Don't you think you could call me Trey?"

Nell laughed. "If I call you Trey, the next thing you know, Tad will be calling you Trey."

Trey laughed with her. "Well, that wouldn't be so bad, would it? He seems to be a very bright and well-mannered boy—someone I wouldn't mind knowing." He paused and looked down at her. "As a matter of fact," he continued, his voice tender, "I don't mind admitting to you that I would also like to know his mother better."

Nell's face was filled with surprise. She looked away, clearly nonplussed.

"I'm sorry. I didn't mean to make you uncomfortable," Trey said softly.

Looking back at him, she gave him a small smile. "That's all right. The truth is, I guess I'd like to know you better, as well. You're a most interesting person."

"You know what I mean, Nell," Trey said quietly.

For a long moment Nell and Trey looked at each other. Without thinking, the gambler reached out and stroked Nell's hair, telling her, "Your hair is so beautiful. I've noticed that when the sun strikes it, it almost looks as though it's on fire." He smiled knowingly. "It seems most appropriate, because I get the feeling you're a fiery woman, Nell Gentry."

She laughed, and he instinctively leaned toward her until their lips were but inches apart. His hand moved to her shoulder, then to the back of her neck, and he felt her soft, warm skin. Putting his arms around her, Trey gently urged Nell's body against his. He bent his head, and for a brief moment their lips touched.

Then Nell suddenly pulled away and stepped back, and the gambler inwardly sighed. He knew that the beautiful woman standing an arm's length away from him had been longing for him as much as he had been longing for her, and he was startled by the depth of his feelings for her. It had been many years since he had allowed himself to be close to a woman in anything more than a purely physical way—no one, in fact, since Deborah—and he wondered if there had been anyone in the interval since Nell's husband had died.

She was staring at him, and he could almost feel the struggle within her. The attraction between them was powerful, and he was sure that she felt the same degree of desire for him as he was feeling for her. "Nell . . ." he whispered, his voice hoarse.

Nell shook her head and then looked around to make sure no one had seen them. "We . . . we shouldn't have done that."

He wondered how much of her hesitation was because he was a gambler—which was not exactly the most respectable of professions, after all. And he also found himself wondering whether, if he were to alter his way of living, she would find him suitable.

Trey was about to speak when Luke Hightower suddenly called from the other side of the stage, "Okay, folks! Let's get back on the coach. We've got about five miles to go before we make camp for the night."

I may surprise you, Nell Gentry, Trey Farnsworth said to himself as he helped the beautiful redhead back into the coach. *And I may surprise myself as well.*

On a trail alongside the Powder River, on the opposite side of the mountains from the mining road, Zeke Slade and his men awaited the stagecoach. It had been scheduled to pass by about two hours before sunset, and though it was not as yet completely dark, the sun had been down for almost an hour, and the stage had still not shown.

Jim Silverthorn walked over to a yucca plant and began to relieve himself.

"Hey, just what the hell do you think you're doin' there, Silverthorn? Floodin' the valley?" Bill Kelly asked, to the amusement of the others.

"Nah, he's just waterin' the lilies, that's all," Luther Murdock quipped, and again the comment was greeted with laughter.

Finishing, Silverthorn buttoned his pants and turned toward the others. "Seems to me like you could think of somethin' more serious to be concerned with than me answerin' a call of nature," he grumbled.

"Like what?"

"Well, like where the hell is the stage?" he asked. "We been hangin' aroun' here practically all day."

"It'll be here," Slade muttered.

"That's what you been sayin' for hours," Silverthorn complained. "Hell, there ain't no stage comin' through this way. If there was, it would've been here by now."

"Maybe Silverthorn's right. Maybe the stage ain't gonna come," Slim Hawkins remarked.

Zeke Slade spat into the dust and then growled, "If it's come every other time, what makes you think it won't come this time?"

"Well, maybe we shouldn't have killed them people back at the way station," Silverthorn suggested.

"What did you want to do? Leave them alive so they could warn the stage that we're here?" Slade asked.

"What I'm sayin' is maybe we done just that anyhow," Silverthorn suggested. "If they got there and seen everybody dead, don't you think they got a mite suspicious?"

Slade ran a nervous hand through his lank hair. "I don't know," he admitted. "All right," he finally said. "I'll tell you what. Let's go back along the trail and see if we can maybe find out what's happened to them."

"How far back do you think we ought to go?" Silverthorn asked.

"If need be, we'll ride all the way back to the way station."

"I don't know, Slade. You really want to go there?" Slim asked. "I mean, we left three dead men there."

"So we left three dead men there. So what? They wasn't no problem to handle when they was alive, what makes you worry about 'em now that they're dead?"

"It ain't that. It's just that . . . well, what if there's someone there askin' questions?" Slim queried.

"If they ask the wrong questions, we'll kill 'em," Slade said simply. "But I aim to find out what's happened to that damned stagecoach."

The travelers went another five miles, and the stagecoach once again rolled to a halt. Up top, Luke Hightower pointed to a grassy area between the road and a fast-running stream and said, "The place I picked out to camp is just down at the bottom of this here hill."

He then scratched his beard, adding, "Only thing was, I never figured on it bein' this hard to get to."

Luke, Dingo, Nate, and Clint were looking at the obstacle that lay between them and what was to be their camp. About three hundred yards down the hill from the coach, the road suddenly curved to the right and then narrowed to what looked to be an impassable degree.

Setting the brake on the stage, Luke and Dingo walked down to look at the area. They stayed down there for a long time, talking and gesturing, and finally Clint, Nate, and Trey walked down to join them.

Clint asked Luke the question that was on everyone's mind. "What do you think? Can we make it through here all right?"

"Not any way that I can figure," the driver answered. "In fact, unless there's another route through here that I don't know about, we're just about stumped." Turning to the young prisoner, Luke queried, "Nate, how about you? You know any other way through these mountains other than this here road?"

"No, I don't," Nate replied glumly. Folding his arms across his chest, he studied the roadbed and then said, "I've been here before, Luke, but I swear I don't remember the road being this narrow."

"Could be some of it got washed out," Dingo suggested. "Some of the rains in these here mountains are real gully washers. If the road ain't bein' used real regular, why it can start crumblin' away without anyone knowin' nothin' about it."

"I guess it don't matter if that's the case or not, 'cause it looks like we got no choice but to turn around and go back," Luke declared.

"Wait a minute," Trey put in. "Are you saying now that we should double back and then go up the other side of this mountain range, as originally planned?"

"I don't see any other way to do it than that way," Luke confirmed, shrugging.

"If we go back the other way, how long will that delay us in reaching Buffalo?" the gambler asked.

"It would add a whole day, I'm sure. Maybe a day and a half," Luke answered.

Trey shook his head. "Gentlemen, we can't do that. If we add one more day to the schedule, that boy back there is going to die."

"Now, hold on here, fella! Where do you get off saying something like that?" Luke asked. "You can't be sure about that."

"I'm afraid I am."

"What makes you so sure?" the driver asked, his voice mocking. "Is it your gambling instinct?"

"No, Mr. Hightower," Trey replied solemly. "Unfortunately, this isn't a gamble. Take my word for it. If we don't get to Buffalo in a reasonable length of time, that boy is going to die. I haven't said anything to his mother, because I don't want to alarm her, but I am absolutely certain that Tad has an inflamed appendix—and if it ruptures, he will die. He may, of course, die anyway, even under a doctor's care, but if we could get him to Buffalo and a competent medical practitioner, he would at least have a fighting chance."

"Now, dammit, mister, you can't just come right out and make a statement like that . . . like maybe you're the high and mighty, or something," Luke said, exasperated. "You don't know for sure that that boy's goin' to die."

"Luke," Clint Townsend said quietly. "For what it's worth, I agree with Mr. Farnsworth. I don't know anything about rupturing appendixes or anything like that, so I can't say that that is what's troubling the boy. But in my time I've seen death on a lot of faces—and

I'm seein' it on that boy's face now. And if you think about it, you'll have to admit that you see it there, too."

"Damn!" Luke swore and then sighed. "All right. All right. Maybe I just didn't want to see it," he confessed. "Okay. We'll go through. I don't even know how we're going to get the stage to the bottom of this hill—and if we do make it to the bottom of this one, who's to say we won't find another one just as bad tomorrow? But somehow we'll get this coach through, all the way to Buffalo."

"Maybe we ought to just camp up at the top of the hill for the night," Dingo suggested. "Then we can figure out a way to tackle this road first thing in the morning."

"No, we may as well go ahead and try and get the stage down tonight," Luke countered. "It ain't gonna be no easier tomorrow."

Trey Farnsworth studied the problematic section of road. A sheer rock wall about ten feet high bordered the right side of the road, while on the left there was a sharp drop of twenty to thirty feet. Dingo measured how wide it was from the wall to the drop off, finding it was almost exactly the same width as the distance between the wheels of the coach. There was a variance of perhaps as little as three inches between staying on the road and dropping the outside wheel rims over the edge. Adding to that the curve of the road, it meant that as the coach went downhill, it would also have to be turned within that tolerance of three inches.

"You know, if that coach tumbles over the side and takes the team with it, we're goin' to lose the horses," Luke remarked as he studied the situation. "Then we'd be set afoot out here. I mean, we could probably haul the damn coach back up, but it wouldn't do us no good with a dead or injured team."

"Yeah, that's true," the lawman agreed.

"Why don't we disconnect all the horses but one?" Dingo suggested. "That way we'd only be riskin' that one."

"Good thinking, Dingo," Nate remarked. "But maybe we could use two. One in front of the coach, and another connected by a rope to the rear. That way the horse at the rear could be used to hold the coach back as it starts down the hill."

Sidney Durant suddenly wandered down the hill and joined the other men. Looking smug, he declared, "Well, it looks like I was right after all, doesn't it? You have no choice now but to go back to the junction of Powder Creek and Willow Creek, then head up the other side of the mountains where there is a *decent* road."

"We aren't going back," Luke said. "We're going ahead."

"What? You plan to go ahead through here? Why, that's preposterous!" Durant sputtered. "It's more than preposterous, it's . . . it's insane! And it is impossible!"

"Thanks for your opinion, Mr. Durant," Luke snickered. He then looked at the others, asking, "Does anybody have any good ideas?"

"I think I know how we can do it," Trey suggested quietly.

"You!" Durant hooted. "Oh, that's a good one. First you play doctor, now you are going to play stage driver. Tell me, Mr. Farnsworth, just what makes you think you can drive a stage?"

"Oh, I don't think I can drive it," Trey replied. "It takes quite a bit of skill to handle a team and coach like this, and I know absolutely nothing about driving a stage. But I do understand mathematics and geometry. And that is the key that can get us out of here . . . if you would be interested in hearing it, Luke."

The driver threw up his hands. "Since I got no

ideas of my own, I'd be more than willing to listen to what you got."

"What?" Durant shouted. "Are you actually going to give credence to this gambler? This is absolutely unbelievable! Turn the coach around! Turn around, I say, and take us up the other side of the mountains as you were supposed to. I'll not risk this money and my life in some crazy scheme concocted by a gambler!"

"Mr. Durant, I told you before and I'll tell you again," Luke Hightower said evenly. "We ain't holdin' you a prisoner. If you don't want to ride along with the rest of us on this here coach, why, you're free to get off right here and right now."

Durant looked around at the distant hills and mountains, vast and empty of any suggestion of civilization other than their own tiny pocket of humanity. "I'd be a fool to start out on my own out here," he retorted. "I've no idea where I am or which way to go. It would be suicide."

"Then you got no choice but to go along with the rest of us," Luke observed. "And if you can't say nothin' to help us out, then, damn your hide, don't you say nothin' at all!"

"I'll remember that, Hightower!" Durant snapped, pointing his finger at the driver. "I'll remember every word of it!"

"Oh, I'm sure you will, Mr. Durant. I'm sure you will." Shaking his head, he turned to the gambler. "Okay, what's this here mathematical idea of yours?"

"Let me show you." Trey knelt on the ground and then drew a semicircle in the dirt. "Let's say that this arc represents the segment of the road that we now occupy. If we were to carry the arc all the way through, we would have a circle—like so." He demonstrated his point by drawing a complete circle. "Now, all we have to do is determine the distance from the arc to the center of this circle. That would be the radius. If we anchored a rope at the radius and tied the other end onto the stage, we could more or less swing the coach around the arc. Even if the outer wheels slipped over the edge, it wouldn't matter, for the rope would keep it on its predescribed arc."

"I'll be damned," Luke said, grinning broadly. "You know, you just may have somethin' there!" He chuckled and then admitted, "I don't understand half of them words you was sayin', but lookin' at that plan of yours, I can tell that it's gonna work."

Standing, the gambler suggested, "If you gentlemen will tie the rope securely to the coach, I'll pace out enough of the road to determine the circle's radius. That way we'll know exactly how long the rope has to be and where to anchor it." He looked at the craggy wall lining one side of the road and added, "It shouldn't be too difficult to find the perfect boulder to use as the anchor."

"Then let's do it," Clint suggested, and he, Dingo, and Luke started back up to the coach to secure the rope, while Trey began pacing off the road. Periodically he would stop and use his pocket watch to measure the angles he needed to determine the radius.

As soon as the calculations were complete, the plan was put into operation. To the satisfaction and amazement of everyone, the coach, securely anchored by the radius rope, swung around the road as easily as if it were a giant pendulum. At one point, one of the rear wheels slipped over the edge, but the rope held the coach firmly in place, and it was a simple matter to guide the wheel back onto the road to continue.

Whooping with glee, Luke exclaimed, "That there experiment almost makes a body want to go back to school and get more learnin'!"

They began making camp, and the shotgunner

remarked to everyone, "I tell you what. I can see why that feller's so good at poker. He's about the smartest feller I ever run across."

After a fire had been started, Clint Townsend stood and shouldered a rifle, saying, "We'll split up the watch during the night. Who want's the second one?"

"I have no intention of standing watch," Sidney Durant complained huffily.

"Mr. Durant," Clint responded, "I have no intention of asking you. I want someone who is dependable."

The men agreed among themselves who would stand watch in what order. With that decided, the rest of the passengers settled down for the night.

Trey Farnsworth walked over to where Nell Gentry was sitting beside her son, who was sleeping fitfully. Kneeling beside her, he said softly, "How is he?"

"Not very well, I'm afraid," she answered, shaking her head slowly.

"Nell, I hope I didn't offend you earlier. I certainly wouldn't want to do that."

She put her hand on his arm. "It's all right. You don't have to apologize. I wasn't offended." She looked into his dark eyes and gave him a small smile. "Truthfully, Trey, you may very well be the most desirable man I have ever known. But I am a responsible, grown woman. I have a child to raise and a hotel to run—though a gambler moving from town to town, and getting run out of many of them, can't possibly understand that kind of responsibility." She sighed, adding, "At any rate, easy as I admit it would be to be swept off my feet by you, I can't afford to give my heart to a gambler. And especially not now. My only concern at this moment is for my son."

He nodded slowly. "I understand. And I want to help in any way that I can."

Tilting her head, she studied him for a long moment, then said, "I do believe you mean that."

"I do. And as a matter of fact, I intend to make good on that promise. I'll go get some water from the stream. A cold compress on Tad's forehead may help bring his fever down somewhat."

Before Nell could respond, Trey stood and grabbed the water bucket that sat nearby and then hurried off.

Several miles south of where they had waited, Zeke Slade and his men reached the Willow River junction. There, by the light of the full moon, they saw the tracks made by the coach and realized why it had not shown up when it was supposed to.

"Will you look at this?" Slade shouted angrily. "They went up the west side of the mountains! Now why do you suppose they did that?"

"Probably 'cause somehow they got wind that we're after them," Silverthorn said, his voice filled with scorn.

Ignoring the jibe, Slade smiled broadly. "Well, what do you know? They probably thought they fooled us good. Like as not they're halfway up the valley now, drinkin' coffee and celebratin' how they put one over on old Zeke Slade. That's good, that's good. They'll think they've won now, so they won't be none too alert." He snorted and then added, "Get ready, fellas. We're gonna come down on them like a duck on a June bug."

Chapter Eight

Sweeping over the travelers' campsite, the cool night breeze was so slight that the nearby trees did no more than whisper with its passing, but it felt pleasant against Nate Yeager's skin as he stood watch. In the distance, a coyote barked and then was answered by the long plaintive howl of another. Overhead, white stars blazed bright, seeming big and close.

Nate got up and tossed a chunk of wood onto the campfire. The fire was kept low so as not to be too visible, but Clint had decided they would be able to keep a low-burning fire, because they were down in a valley ringed by mountains. To see the fire, an observer would have to be on top of one of the surrounding mountains, though if the flames burned too brightly, its reflection could be seen from quite a distance, even from as far as another mountain range.

After watching the fire for a few moments to make certain it did not flare up, Nate then decided to walk to the edge of the stream. He passed the team where they were tied, and in the darkness, they appeared to be moving shadows within shadows. Standing by the edge of the stream, he looked across and into the trees, where a galaxy of tiny golden stars winked on and off—fireflies winging their way in the evening air.

Nate's mind drifted back to the conversation he had had earlier with Shannon McBride, when he learned that the love he felt for her was not merely one-sided. If he understood what she was saying to him, and he believed he did, she loved him, too. And she had been just as confused—and had felt just as guilty—as he had because of it.

The young prisoner was sure that Shannon had never given Cole the least reason to doubt her love, even though she had loved Nate instead. Now, although Cole was dead and buried, he continued to come between them because the guilt Shannon had felt for loving her fiancé's brother was just as strong as it had been when Cole was alive. Nate told himself that if he were honest with himself, he would admit that he felt a bit of that guilt as well.

A scuffling sound interrupted Nate's thoughts, and he turned, his gun held at the ready. The tall, solid form of Clint Townsend was coming toward him.

"I saw you leave the camp and come down here," the lawman said. "Is everything all right?"

"Yes. I just felt like stretching my legs a bit," Nate answered.

Clint stroked his chin and looked back toward the encampment. "What do you think, Nate? Will Zeke Slade hit us tonight?"

"I don't know," Nate admitted. "I have no doubt that he'll hit us during our trip—if not tonight, then certainly at some point before we reach Buffalo. He knows about the money, and he's damn well not about to let it get away from him."

"If he does hit us, it should prove to be a very interesting experience," Clint remarked wryly.

"Interesting? How do you mean?" Nate asked,

regarding the lawman curiously. "That's a rather strange way of putting it."

Shrugging, the sheriff declared, "What I mean is, we've got ourselves quite a traveling circus here, wouldn't you say? Look at this group. We have a widow, a spoiled young girl, a sick little boy, a dude gambler, a jackass banker, a crusty stage driver—who's about ready to strangle the banker—a sawed-off shotgun guard, and you . . . an escaped prisoner."

"You left yourself out, Sheriff."

"Ah, yes," Clint responded, his tone ironic. "Well, I am the prize among us all. I am the sheriff, the one responsible for the protection of our little band, and I"—he paused for a long moment before he drew a deep breath and went on—"I am a coward."

"A coward? How can you say such a thing? You won the Medal of Honor—and unless I am sorely mistaken, the Medal of Honor isn't given for cowardice."

"Oh, yes, there is the medal, isn't there?" Clint mused, sighing. Folding his arms across his chest, he noted, "Well, let's just start with that, shall we? That medal has marked me ever since . . . *branding* me a hero, when the truth is, awarding it to me was the biggest joke the Army has ever pulled."

"You mean you didn't earn it? You weren't on that water detail?"

"Oh, yes, I was a member of the water detail. I did go down to the creek with the other men that day . . . Reno's Creek they call it now, though I imagine a few thousand Sioux have their own name for it. And like the others on the detail, I carried a dozen empty canteens, and I filled them with water."

"But that was dangerous, wasn't it?" Nate asked. "You aren't saying that no one on that detail deserved the medal, are you?"

"Oh, it was dangerous all right, and every man on

that detail faced the danger bravely. You see, the Indians knew we would be needing water, and they were watching the stream closely. But getting down to the water and coming back alive was a matter of survival, that's all." He was silent for a long moment before continuing, "What the citation doesn't speak of is what I did earlier, when we crossed the stream to attack the village."

"What did you do?"

"I tucked my tail between my legs and I ran," Clint admitted. Squatting by the stream, he plunged his cupped hands in the water and scooped some up. He drank a little, splashed some on his face and then stood up and pulled a handkerchief from his pocket and wiped his face and hands before he continued the story.

"Clint, you don't have to tell me this," Nate said softly.

Shaking his head, Clint replied, "Nate, I've never told this story to a living soul, and it's haunted me ever since that June afternoon thirteen years ago. Now I want to tell it. I *need* to tell it."

Nate nodded. "I understand."

"I was a sergeant, attached to Major Reno's command," the lawman explained. "We received the order to attack the lower end of the village, and Custer was going to attack the upper end. The idea was to sweep through the village and meet in the middle."

"I take it that was before you knew how many Indians there were?"

"Oh, Custer knew, all right," Clint growled. "He just didn't give a damn. He thought he was invincible and could whip the whole Sioux Nation. I guess we did, too, because we started out in grand style. We crossed the river at a gallop and then charged toward the Indian village." Snorting derisively, Clint said mockingly, "Did I say village? It was a city, with every man, woman, and child armed and sworn to kill us. Halfway through our charge we realized that we weren't attacking, we were being attacked! Mounted and heavily armed Indians, five or six times our number, were coming toward us!

"We headed into a nearby gulley, and there Reno gave us the order to dismount. *Dismount!* I couldn't believe my ears! We were cavalry troopers, trained to fight from the saddle. Besides, when we dismounted, one in four had to hold the horses, so we immediately decreased our fighting force by twenty-five percent."

Nate kept silent as the lawman went on. "Reno was confused, and he kept giving contradictory orders. The officers and scouts around him were trying to convince him to remount and withdraw. One of the scouts was Bloody Knife, our most dependable—and my personal friend. Suddenly a bullet hit Bloody Knife in the face. It was a big one, either a huge ball fired from an old fowling piece or a fifty-caliber slug from something like a Sharps buffalo gun. Bloody Knife's head simply exploded— and blood and bone and brain matter splattered all over my face."

Unconsciously, Clint wiped his face with the hand-kerchief he was holding. "I didn't wait for any further commands. I jumped on my horse and started back for the river. A few seconds later I heard Reno give the order to retreat, and the others came after me. I was the first one across the river and the first one to find a hole in the bluffs on the other side. But the funny thing is *no one knew I had run!* I had panicked, Nate, like a greenhorn private under fire for the first time . . . and nobody realized it, because the order for retreat came immediately afterward."

The big lawman looked down at his hands. "Later, when I learned I was going to be given a medal for getting the water, I tried to tell them I didn't deserve it. They thought I was just being modest, because I couldn't tell them what I had done at the gulley. I took the medal, under what to me were false pretenses, and when my enlistment was up, I got out of the Army."

The two men were quiet for a few seconds. Then Nate broke the silence, asking, "Clint, the order to retreat came almost immediately after you started to run, didn't it?"

"Yes, it did."

"Then you might say that the difference between running and retreating was a matter of rank."

"What do you mean?"

"You said yourself that Reno was confused and giving conflicting orders. Well, when he finally got his senses back, he ordered a retreat—something you already knew was necessary. If you had been a major and Reno a sergeant, then what you did wouldn't have been the running of a coward, it would have been the strategic withdrawal of a military commander."

Clint was lost in thought for a moment. Then he abruptly squeezed Nate's shoulder with a strong hand. "Maybe you're right," he said, a small smile on his face. "I guess I never thought of it quite like that before. Thanks." Stretching, he declared, "Well, I guess maybe I ought to go back up there and try and get a little sleep. My watch is at midnight."

He started for the camp and then stopped and looked back at Nate. "I hope some way we're able to prove your innocence, son. But if we can't, I'm going to have to send you back to prison."

"I hope it doesn't come to that, Clint," Nate replied. "Because I'm not going back."

"Are you saying you would fight me?" the lawman asked.

"If need be," the young prisoner confessed with a nod.

The sheriff smiled thinly and then drew an audible

breath. "Well, my friend, if it does reach the point that there's a showdown between us, I guess we'll learn once and for all, won't we?"

"Learn what?"

"Whether my action at Little Bighorn was the running of a coward or the strategic withdrawal of a military commander."

Shannon McBride was restlessly shifting on her blanket near the fire when she saw Clint Townsend come back into the camp, then lie down. Within a few moments Clint Townsend was snoring contentedly, as were all the others. The young woman envied them, for they had been able to fall asleep quickly, whereas she was still trying to find a position that was comfortable.

She turned over for what had to be the hundredth time and stared out toward the creek bank. She could make out Nate Yeager standing there, illuminated by the full moon, sometimes looking all around the horizon and other times just staring at the water. She wondered what he was thinking about. More specifically, she wondered if he was thinking about her.

Shannon continued to toss and turn, but no matter how hard she tried, sleep refused to come. Finally she sat up and watched the campfire for a few moments; then she decided to take a little walk. She assumed she would be safe as long as she stayed well within sight and sound of the encampment.

She noiselessly made her way down to the creek bank, most of her way lighted by the glow of the small campfire, stopping upstream somewhat from Nate and unseen by him. Walking to the edge of the water, she watched the rushing water, splashing a brilliant white where it broke over the rocks.

The air caressed her skin like fine silk, carrying on it a hint of woodsmoke and coffee. She suddenly wondered whether anyone was near; if so, they would be able to smell the encampment even if they could not see the flames from the fire. Putting the thought from her mind as she pulled her shawl tighter around her shoulders, she looked around as her eyes adjusted to the darkness.

The night sky looked like blue velvet, and the stars glistened like diamonds, while in the distance, barely visible mountain peaks rose in great and mysterious dark slabs against the midnight sky. An owl landed nearby and his wings made a soft whir as he flew by.

If Shannon still had any doubts about abandoning her original intention to return to Boston, this night put them to rest. Despite the dangers they were facing—or, though she could scarcely admit this to herself, because of them— she had never felt so alive.

Glancing to her right, she saw a large, flat rock, and she walked over and sat. Pulling her knees up under her chin, she stared out at the water, and the constant gurgling of the brook soothed her while she sat in contemplative silence.

She thought back a few hours, when she and Nell Gentry had sat talking by the fire. The two women had discussed Trey Farnsworth, and Shannon was sure she had detected something in Nell that had not been there earlier in the day. There was a sparkle in her eyes when she spoke of Trey, but when Shannon questioned her about it, the redhead insisted it was merely that she was so touched by the gambler's compassion—not something one would expect to find in someone of his profession.

Shannon, on the other hand, was more impressed with Trey's wealth of knowledge about music, literature, and art—subjects she would never have expected a gambler to understand, much less know. She prided herself on her fine Boston education, yet the two of them had wiled away many of the hours during the long journey discussing the works of various artists, writers, and composers, and it had been clear that the gambler not only knew his subjects well, but he held interesting opinions on them. It had also been clear to her that Trey's background was not that of the rough-and-tumble wanderer, and she was very sure that he was much deeper than he appeared to be.

"It's not a good idea for you to wander away from the camp like this," a voice suddenly declared. "Though I'll confess I'm glad you did."

Shannon had been so absorbed in her own thoughts that she had neither seen nor heard Nate Yeager approach her. Nevertheless, she was not surprised by his presence. "Aren't you supposed to be on watch?" she asked offhandedly, without looking up from the water.

"I *am* on watch, which explains why I'm here," Nate replied dryly. "What about you?"

"I couldn't sleep."

"You've been traveling hard ever since you left Boston," he observed. "I can't imagine you not being tired enough to sleep."

"Maybe I just have too much on my mind."

He sighed. "I can understand that. I have a lot on my mind, too." His voice softened. "I hope some of it is the same thing."

She still would not look at him. "Nate, what's going to happen to you?"

"What do you mean?"

"As much as I disagree with that awful Mr. Durant, he is right about one thing. You're an escaped prisoner. When we arrive in Buffalo, you'll be sent back to the penitentiary."

"Yeah, that's what Clint Townsend just reminded me," Nate remarked. "But I'll tell you what I told him. I'm not going back."

"How are you going to arrange that?"

"There's no doubt in my mind that Zeke Slade is going to attack the stagecoach somewhere between here and Buffalo. The money we're carrying is as much bait to him as cheese is to a rat. And when he takes the bait, I'm going to take that two-legged rat."

"I see. So your entire plan is based upon capturing Zeke Slade and somehow forcing him to clear you, is that it?"

"That's it," Nate agreed.

"What if it doesn't work out that way?" Shannon asked. "What if you aren't able to capture him?"

"Then I'll figure out some other way. No matter what it takes, Shannon, I am not going back to prison."

"Even if it means running from the law for the rest of your life?"

"Yes," Nate murmured. "If it comes to that, then I'm prepared to do just that."

"That certainly wouldn't be much of a life," she suggested.

"No, it wouldn't be." Nate reached down and put his hand under her chin and then gently turned her face up to look into his own. "That's why I could never ask you to come with me. Before a man would ask a woman to marry him, he should have something to offer her. . . a home, security, and a future."

She felt her face coloring. "Marriage?" she asked, the word catching in her throat.

"Yes," he whispered. "I love you, Shannon McBride. I have always loved you, and I always will."

"Oh, Nate," Shannon said. She was about to protest that such feelings were inappropriate, that she could not reciprocate his desire to marry, but before she could say anything further, Nate lifted her to her feet and pressed his lips against hers.

A tidal wave of pleasure washed over Shannon, and despite all her resolve not to act upon her feelings for him, despite her carefully reasoned logic for staying clear of him, she found herself dissolving under the fire of his kiss. As the intensity of his kiss grew, she pressed her body against his, feeling heat coursing through her as if she had turned to molten metal.

Finally Nate pulled away from her. "Shannon," he began, his voice forceful, "I love you, and I want to know how you feel about me."

The young woman sighed. "I love you, Nate," she confessed in a small voice.

Nate turned away from her then and put his hand to his forehead. "Damn!" he exclaimed.

She gasped in surprise. "What is it? I tell you I love you, and you act as though I've slapped you in the face."

He looked back at her, a bittersweet smile on his lips. "Don't you see it, girl? Now that we can finally tell each other how we really feel, there's nothing we can do about it—unless I can prove my innocence."

"Well, then," Shannon said resolutely, stepping to him and putting her hands on his shoulders, "we shall just have to prove your innocence. Now that I've admitted my love, I don't intend to let you get away from me."

Nate smiled broadly and pulled her to him again, folding her into his arms in a bear hug. "That's all I need to hear," he murmured into her ear. "Shannon, I'm going to get Zeke Slade and make him tell what actually happened that day. If I have to soak my pants in kerosene and ride down to hell to kick the devil in the backside to do it, it's going to be done."

Shannon laughed. "Well, Nate Yeager, I suppose if you insist on doing that, the least I can do is hold the kerosene can for you."

"Deal!" he exclaimed and then sealed their bargain with another kiss.

*   *   *

"The trail goes that way," Zeke Slade insisted, pointing toward the mountains.

"No, it don't. It goes that way, through that pass," Jim Silverthorn replied, pointing in a different direction.

"Dammit, I once held up a mule train over here. I know where the trail is."

"Were they pack mules, or were they pullin' a wagon?"

Slade looked at his man in bewilderment. "Pack mules," he answered.

"Well, there you go," Silverthorn said. "Pack mules can use a mountain trail. A wagon needs a road—and the road goes through that pass."

"The moon's gone down, and it's too dark to make out much from the sign," Slim Hawkins interjected. "Maybe we ought to wait until light and then get a bead on them. I mean, if we strike out down one of these two trails you're arguin' about, and we choose the wrong one, we might lose 'em."

"All right, all right," Slade agreed reluctantly. "We'll stay here till dawn." He pulled off a plug of chewing tobacco and stuck it in his cheek. Scowling, he grumbled, "We're supposed to have a friend on the coach. Why in hell don't we get some kind of a signal?"

Dingo poked at the dying fire with a long stick until the coals that had been glowing broke out into flames. He then tossed a few more chunks of wood onto the fire, and when he was satisfied that they had caught, he sat down on a rock and watched them burn.

His gaze fell on Sidney Durant some thirty feet away from him. The clerk lay sleeping with his arms wrapped securely around the black bag he had carried ever since he had boarded the coach in Medicine Bow. And in that bag was one hundred thousand dollars.

Dingo tried to imagine what one hundred thousand dollars looked like—and how long it would take to spend it. The most money he had ever had at one time was six hundred and thirty dollars—the money he had stolen from the Kansas Stage Line. He had proceeded to lose most of it in a poker game just two days later, and the rest he had spent on women, whiskey, and food.

Dingo smiled. The whiskey had been rotgut, and the whores had been ugly, but the food had been wonderful. After he had been caught and sent to prison, he used to pass the long hours by thinking back on some of the food he had enjoyed during that little spree: steaks, chops, roast beef, and—which he discovered to his great surprise that he liked—mutton. The law had caught up with him as he was leaving a restaurant in Abilene, but the timing had been perfect. He had just spent his last dime.

Thinking about the money in Durant's satchel, the shotgunner smiled again. With that much money—or even a share of it—he could leave the territory and maybe go out to San Francisco or even back East, to someplace like Boston. The law would never think of looking for him back East.

He had heard the beautiful McBride girl talk about what a wonderful place Boston was, and he wondered how many restaurants Boston had—and how long it would take someone to eat his way through all of them. With enough money, it would probably take a long, long time. . . .

Clint Townsend was not sure what caused him to wake up, but he abruptly opened his eyes and lay there for a moment, feeling as if something was wrong. Glancing over toward the stagecoach, he saw that it appeared to be all right as it stood clearly illuminated by the bright orange flames from the campfire. Suddenly he realized that the coach would not be as plain to see as it was unless the campfire was too big. Leaping to his feet, he looked over and saw that the fire was blazing brightly, providing a beacon that could lead anyone— including Zeke Slade and his men—right into the camp.

"What the hell!" Clint bellowed. "Who's on watch here? Who built up this fire?"

Nate Yeager sat up on his blanket and sleepily replied, "Dingo. Dingo's supposed to be on watch."

Dingo had been sound asleep, slumped forward against a log, but the sudden shout woke him.

"Get that fire down!" Clint ordered as he rushed to contain the blaze.

Dingo leapt up and began kicking dirt onto the flames with the sheriff. Brought under control, the fire was once again a small glow rather than a huge blaze.

"Dingo, what the hell were you trying to do? Were you sending a signal to Slade and his men?" the lawman challenged.

"Sheriff, I swear to you, I don't know how that fire got so big," Dingo countered. "I mean, it's true I fell asleep, and there was no excuse for that. But there wasn't enough wood on the fire to allow it to build to such a blaze. I swear it!"

"Then how do you account for the fact that it was just that? Wood doesn't just jump into a fire."

"I admit it looks suspicious," Dingo mumbled. "But I didn't do it."

Shaking his head, a look of skepticism on his face, the lawman muttered, "It'll take more'n just your say-so to convince me, I'm afraid."

The others were all awake now, and Clint Townsend turned away from Dingo and addressed everyone else. "Okay, folks, as long as we're all up, we may as well break camp. It'll* be light soon, and we need to get under way."

Everyone began stirring, rolling up blankets and packing away cooking gear. The women walked down to the stream and splashed water on their faces and then combed their hair.

As they returned to the others, Nell Gentry remarked to Shannon McBride, "I'll be awfully glad when we reach Buffalo and I'll be able to wash my hair. I feel as though there's a peck of trail dust covering it." She gave the young brunette a sidelong glance, adding, "I must say that I'm surprised you're taking our hardships so lightly."

Shannon blushed and looked down at her feet. "Yes, well, I guess perhaps I've discovered that there's more Wyoming than Massachusetts in me after all."

The redhead cocked her head and studied Shannon for a long moment but said nothing. She then walked over to where her son lay on the ground and gathered him into her arms, carrying him over to the stagecoach.

Hurrying to help Nell carry Tad into the coach, Trey Farnsworth was sure that the boy was steadily growing worse. He had checked him as soon as they had been awakened and discovered that the child's fever had increased during the night, as had his pain. As the others busied themselves with loading everything back on the stagecoach, Trey took a bucket and walked down to the stream. There he broke off chunks of the ice that had formed along the edges and filled the bucket with it. By the time he returned to the stage, the team was hitched and the passengers were boarding.

As the coach got under way, the gambler took out his pocketknife and cut a bit of canvas from the window curtain and then began wrapping it around a large chunk of ice. Nate looked at him as if he had lost his mind.

"Trey, what are you doing?" the young prisoner asked, bewilderment written on his face.

"When I get finished with this, it's going to be a most serviceable ice pack. And I'm going to have Mrs. Gentry hold this on Tad's stomach, right about there." He pointed to the lower right side of the boy's abdomen.

Nell looked at him with a questioning expression on her own face. "That seems like a rather strange thing to do," she said. "Tad's in so much discomfort as it is, why would I wish to increase it?"

"Because it'll accomplish two things," the gambler answered. "It'll numb his abdomen so that the pain won't be quite as severe, and it'll slow the infection." He sighed and then told her, "I haven't wanted to alarm you, but I'm convinced he has appendicitis."

"Appendi . . . what?" Nell responded.

"Appendicitis. The appendix is swollen and inflamed. Hopefully the cold will keep it from bursting before we reach Buffalo, but if it does burst, it might help retard the spread of the infection until your Dr. Presnell can perform an appendectomy—that is, remove the appendix. It's a surgical procedure."

"Oh, my God!" Nell exclaimed, putting her hand to her mouth in fright. "That'll be very dangerous, won't it?"

"There's a degree of risk, yes, but it isn't nearly as dangerous as letting the appendix rupture." Trey handed the canvas-covered ice to Nell. "Here, put this on him," he instructed.

Nell lay the ice pack on Tad's stomach, but Tad instantly jumped and cried out in pain. "Oh, Mama, don't! That's so cold, it hurts!"

Nell jerked her hand away, but Trey reached across the space between the seats and put his hand on her wrist. Gently, but firmly, he guided the ice pack back on Tad's stomach. "Keep it there," he ordered. "It will be uncomfortable only briefly, and then he won't feel the cold anymore—nor, hopefully, the pain."

"All right," Nell agreed, although her expression clearly bespoke her uncertainty. She held the ice pack in place, despite the complaints and whimpers of the boy.

"Madam, for the life of me, I can't understand why you insist upon doing everything this man tells you," Sidney Durant said.

"Well, I think she should listen to him," Nate put in. "I don't know anything about doctoring, but it seems to me like most of it is just common sense—and I've never known anybody with more common sense than this man. You saw how he managed to get us down the mountain last night."

"Yes, I saw. It was a damn fool stunt that could've gotten us all killed," Durant sputtered.

"It was a very smart feat," the young prisoner corrected, his blue eyes flashing. "I wouldn't call it a stunt at all."

There were murmurs of agreement from the other passengers. Then Trey turned to Nell and looked her intently in the eyes. "I don't mean to force you to do anything you don't want to do."

"Nonsense, I trust you," Nell responded.

I trust you! The words were like a dagger in Trey Farnsworth's heart, for they were the same words uttered by Deborah before he operated on her... before he *killed* her.

For a moment, Trey almost told Nell Gentry to take the ice pack away. After all, who was he to give advice? He had walked away from the responsibility of his Hippocratic oath. He was no longer a doctor—not in the eyes of the world and certainly not in his own eyes. But just as he was about to say something, Tad spoke.

"Mr. Farnsworth was right, Mama. I don't feel it anymore, and my stomach's quit hurting."

"There, that's excellent," the gambler said, sighing with relief that the numbing had taken effect so quickly.

Nell put her free hand on Trey's. "How can I ever thank you for what you've done for my son? I owe you a great deal."

Putting his other hand over hers, Trey remarked, "Nonsense. You don't owe me a thing. I'm glad I was able to help you, Nell—you and Tad both. I'd like to get to know him better, after all."

The two of them looked at each other for a long moment. Then Nell blushed and pulled her hand from Trey's. Obviously embarrassed, the redhead glanced at each of the other passengers, but the only one who was watching her was Shannon McBride, and she had a conspiratorial smile on her face.

The stagecoach had been traveling for about a half hour when Nate Yeager stared more intently out the window. Something had caught the corner of his eye, and as he looked, he saw it again. It was a patch of reflected light, playing along the rocks. Puzzled, he leaned out the window and looked up and then saw that it was Dingo's rifle, flashing in the sun.

"Hold it! Hold it!" he shouted.

"Whoa!" Luke Hightower called to the team, and with a squeak of brakes, the coach came to a halt.

Nate flung open the door and leapt out, standing with his hands on his hips and staring up at the box.

"What is it?" Clint Townsend asked from his position atop the stage.

"It's Dingo's rifle," Nate answered. "Look over there on the rocks."

Clint, Luke, and Dingo looked in the direction that Nate indicated. Then the shotgun guard jiggled the rifle in his grip, and the patch of light danced around before them.

"Dammit, Dingo, what the hell are you doing?" Luke asked.

"Get that rifle wrapped in something, Dingo!" Clint ordered. "The way that thing's flashing, someone could see us for twenty miles."

"Hell, I'm sorry!" Dingo yelped, reaching quickly for his duster. "I'll keep a watch on it. It won't happen again."

"It better not," the lawman growled. "First there was the fire, now this. What's next? Smoke signals?"

They got back on the road, with Nate keeping an eye peeled out the window. Not ten minutes passed when a rifle shot abruptly rang out, followed by the whine of bullets.

"Nate!" Clint shouted from atop the coach. "They're here! They're behind us!"

"Move over, Clint, I'm coming up top!" Nate shouted back. As he threw open the door, he looked at the other passengers and instructed, "Slade and his men'll be shooting high—at us. Trey, put the boy and the women on the floor, and you and Durant lie down in the seats."

"I can shoot as well, you know," Trey yelled over the gunshots coming from up top.

"Are you any good?"

"Not very."

Nate shook his head. "Then don't bother. If they see that shooting's coming from down in the coach, they'll shoot back. Let us handle it."

Reaching for the luggage rack, Nate pulled himself up on top of the stage. By now Luke had whipped the horses into a dead run, and the coach was bouncing and lurching at full speed along the little-used wagon road. Dingo had left his place in the driver's box and positioned himself on the coach top with the sheriff. Joining the others, who lay as flat as they could and still take aim, Nate began shooting back at the attackers.

A bullet whizzed by Nate's ear, and he immediately flattened himself against the coach top.

"How many are there?" Nate shouted at Clint.

"I've seen five!" the lawman yelled.

"Yeah, that's what was at his camp!" the prisoner confirmed.

The wheels of the coach were throwing up dust, which made it difficult to see clearly enough to get a good shot. But it made it just as difficult for Zeke Slade and his men to see the defenders.

Nate Yeager got to his knees to take aim when suddenly the coach hit a deep wagon rut, and he was thrown off balance. He found himself hanging over the side of the luggage rack, his face precariously close to the wheel. Grabbing desperately for something to hold on to, his hand found the sidelight, and he gripped it with all his might while dust and rocks were thrown up into his face. Closing his eyes, he found that made the sensation even worse. Then a bullet fired by one of Slade's men zinged close to his head, and he instinctively ducked.

"Hang on, Nate!" Clint shouted. "We'll get you up!"

While Dingo kept up the shooting, the muscular lawman hurried to the young prisoner's aid. Nate felt himself being lifted up by the seat of his pants and hauled to safety.

"Whew, boy!" Clint shouted. "Don't do that again!"

Nate grinned. "I'll try not to!" he promised.

Repositioning themselves, Nate and Clint resumed the defense.

Dingo fired, and Nate saw one of Slade's men grab his right knee as blood poured through his pant leg. Then Clint got off a good shot, and another one of the gang grabbed his stomach and then tumbled backward off his horse.

Suddenly Zeke Slade called to his men, "Fall back! Fall back!" The robbers then abruptly all reined in their horses while the stagecoach continued on ahead.

"We did it!" Clint Townsend shouted triumphantly.

"Yeah," Nate responded, "but for how long?"

"Dammit, Slade, they're gettin' away!" Jim Silverthorn said.

"And with our money," Slim Hawkins added.

"Just hold on, boys," Slade responded, looking at his men. Slim and Silverthorn were uninjured, but Bill Kelly was white as a sheet from the pain of his shattered kneecap, and his right leg was covered with blood from the knee down. Luther Murdock was lying facedown and unmoving in the dirt about a quarter of a mile back, and Slade was sure he was dead.

"What'd we stop for?" Silverthorn asked.

"There's too many of them bastards for us to take them this way," Slade told him. "Who'd have thought they'd have that many guns?"

"Well, you ain't just gonna let the money get away, are you?"

"Naw," Slade replied, a slow smile working its way over his hard face. "Don't forget, we got us a friend on that coach. I figure if we'll just hang back a bit, he'll get it stopped for us." He chuckled, adding, "Why work so hard when we don't have to?"

Chapter Nine

"**L**uke! Hold it up, Luke!" Dingo shouted forward to the driver. "Slade and his bunch have pulled back! You can stop the team now!"

Looking back over his shoulder, Luke Hightower verified that the outlaws had withdrawn. "Whoa, horses!" he yelled, hauling back on the reins and pushing the brake lever forward with his foot. The stage squeaked and rattled to a halt, sitting on the lumber road surrounded by a cloud of dirt and dust that had been thrown up by the gallop. Completely exhausted by their effort and their bodies covered with foam and sweat, the horses stood shuddering in their harness with their chests heaving and breathing loudly.

"My God, listen to those poor critters," Luke declared in a pained voice. His weathered face wore a worried look as he continued, "Damn me if it doesn't just kill my soul to do this to them." Then he smiled, asking, "Weren't they magnificent, though? They gave us all they had—and this after they'd pulled us for two days before I put them to this runnin'. But they're plumb wore out now. If I don't give them a short rest, they're gonna drop dead in their traces, every last one of 'em."

"Go ahead and give them a rest," Clint Townsend agreed, shifting around on the top of the stagecoach so that he was facing forward. "I think Zeke Slade's had enough. I don't think we'll be seein' anything else from him. Not now, anyway." He grinned and then remarked, "After all, we kinda narrowed his odds."

"I wouldn't be giving up on him just yet, Clint," Nate Yeager cautioned, wiping a forearm across his thick sandy hair to keep the sweat from running down into his eyes. "Maybe he won't hit us head on, but you'd be making a big mistake if you believe he's given up. I can't see Zeke Slade just walking away from all this money without attempting another try."

"Well, don't worry, I'm not going to let my guard down, if that's what you mean. But I think we hurt him pretty bad, and I figure ol' Slade is going to have to lick his wounds for a bit. He needs this time about as much as we need it to let our horses blow."

"I'll admit that we probably bought ourselves a little time," Nate said. "You might even say we won the battle . . . though the war isn't over yet." He lay his rifle down. "If you don't mind, Sheriff, I'm going to hop down and have a look at the folks inside the coach. Slade and his boys threw a lot of lead at us. I want to make sure nobody got hit by a stray bullet."

"Yeah, that's a good idea. Especially the boy. I'm mighty worried about that little tyke."

"Yeah, me, too." Nate dropped down to the ground and then opened the door and looked inside.

"Any bullets come through here?" he asked, looking directly at Shannon McBride, his eyes filled with concern.

"No bullets. Just dirt," Shannon answered as she ran her hands over her face.

"Yeah, I guess I can see that," Nate said dryly.

The passengers in the coach looked as if they had all been wallowing like hogs, for they were coated with the same thin film of gray-brown that now covered the stage—dirt and dust that had been thrown up by the hooves and wheels during the mad dash just completed. Sidney Durant, drawn up in the front left corner of the coach, was clutching a handkerchief to his nose.

"I guess it got a little rough for you folks, but we couldn't help it. Is everybody all right?" Nate asked.

"No, we are not all right!" Durant replied testily, his fingers smoothing his small clipped mustache. "That fool driver nearly broke our necks with that wild ride he just gave us!"

"You're still alive, aren't you, mister?" the young prisoner snapped.

"Barely."

"Well, barely's better'n dead. You should be thankful. Believe me, you wouldn't even be that if Slade had caught up with us."

"I disagree. In fact, I think we should stop and wait for Slade to come to us," Durant said.

"What? You think we should stop and wait for him? What's the matter with you, mister? Are you crazy?" Nate asked, dumbfounded.

"Not in the least. In fact, I believe myself to be the only sane person around here. Perhaps if we stop the coach and approach Slade under a flag of truce, we could negotiate with him."

"Negotiate? Negotiate for what?" Nate asked, his voice rising.

"Why, negotiate for our lives, of course," Durant replied. "I have some degree of experience in business negotiations. . . . I am a banker, after all. I would be more than glad to represent our side in this matter. I know that the only thing Slade wants is the money. If we simply give it to him, I'm sure he would ride away

and leave us alone. I don't believe he would kill us
without any reason."

"Those men we buried back at the Powder River
way station might disagree with you, Mr. Durant,"
Nate retorted. "And anyway, you're the one carrying the
money, so that means you're the one Zeke Slade and his
gang are after. I would think you'd appreciate our
fighting them off more than anyone."

"Yes, well, whereas I am carrying the money, it is,
after all, the Medicine Bow Bank's money and not
mine," Durant corrected.

Nate ran an impatient hand through his dust-
coated hair. "It may be the bank's money, but you do
have some responsibility for it."

"I have some responsibility, of course, but I think
we have made an adequate attempt to defend it," the
fussy little clerk countered. "We have fought well, and
there would be no dishonor in surrendering to Slade's
demands. Indeed, I know of no code of honor that
would require us to die for one hundred thousand
dollars of someone else's money."

"No, Mr. Durant, I don't reckon you would know
of such a code of honor," Nate barked. "But then, what
difference would it make? I'm not sure someone like
you would abide by any such rules anyway."

"Sir! Are you accusing me of being a man without
honesty?" Durant demanded.

"No. Just a man without honor," Nate replied.
"And in my book, you can't have one without the other."

He looked over at Nell Gentry then, dismissing
the unpleasant Sidney Durant. Nell was holding Tad's
head on her lap, Shannon was holding the boy's feet,
while Trey Farnsworth was kneeling between the seats,
with his hand resting on Tad's stomach.

"The sheriff wants to know how the boy's doing,"
the prisoner asked. "And I'd like to know myself."

Studying Tad, Nate was not at all reassured by the child's appearance. His face was very pale, and it was obvious that he was hurting badly.

"The ride we just took didn't help things much," Trey replied.

"I'm sorry about the ride, there was nothing—"

The gambler held up his hand, cutting off Nate's apology. "No, no, don't start apologizing. I know it couldn't be helped. I was just making an observation, I wasn't complaining." He pulled Tad's shirt back down and then took his seat, looking across at Nell.

"How is he?" she asked anxiously.

"There's no doubt that the boy is in a great deal of discomfort," the gambler replied. Then he smiled. "However, from everything I can determine, any pain he's feeling now is from the banging around of the rough ride. I'm almost positive that his appendix hasn't burst."

"Good," Nell breathed. Then she tilted her head and stared intently at Trey. "I mean, I think that's good, isn't it?"

"Oh, yes," he assured her. "That's good." He reached down into the bucket and pulled out another chunk of ice. "I sure do wish we had some more ice though," he said as he wrapped the chunk in the canvas. "I'm afraid this is our last piece." He handed it across to Nell.

Just then Clint Townsend climbed down from the top of the coach and stood beside Nate, looking in through the doorway.

"No damages in here," Nate reported.

"Good," the sheriff declared. "Come on, son. Let's hike back along the road a piece and see if we can get an idea as to where Slade might be."

"All right," Nate agreed, and the two men started walking.

"How's the boy doing?" Clint asked.

"Well, according to Trey, whatever it is that's ailing the boy hasn't burst, and that's supposed to be a good sign," Nate answered. Then he shook his head, adding, "But he's in a lot of pain."

"Poor kid," Clint said, sighing. "I wish we could just give him a nice, smooth ride on in to the doctor." His clear blue eyes turned cold. "It really makes me furious, Slade putting a child through all this."

"Zeke Slade never has been known as a compassionate man," Nate observed. "It makes no difference to him whether he's dealing with a man, woman, or child—everyone is treated equally brutally."

When they were far enough away from the coach to ensure that they could not be overheard, the lawman and his prisoner turned and looked back at the others. Luke was up at the front of the team, examining his horses, and Dingo was leaning nonchalantly against the side of the coach, cradling his rifle in his arms. Durant was the only passenger who had left the coach, and he was walking around nervously, stretching his legs.

Looking back at Nate, the sheriff told him, "I want to talk to you about Dingo."

"Dingo? What about him?"

"Turns out, Dingo served some time ago in Kansas. And it was for robbing a stagecoach."

"How do you know this?"

"Soon after he started working for the Wyoming Express Company, I found an old wanted poster on him," Clint explained. "Naturally, I checked up on him, but I learned that he wasn't wanted anymore. He had served his time and got a full release."

"I see. Did you tell the stagecoach people?"

"No," Clint replied, shaking his head. Then he sighed. "I know, I know, I probably should have. But I sort of like Dingo, cantankerous old sort that he is, and I figured he had already paid society whatever debt he owed. If he was trying to make an honest living now, I didn't want to do anything that would cause him problems. Besides, I figure since the stagecoach company never asked anything about him, it wasn't my place to volunteer any information."

Bending, Nate picked up a rock and started tossing it from hand to hand. "How has he worked out?"

"Pretty well. From all I hear, Dingo's been one of their best employees—at least, he has been till now. Tell me, Nate, do you think he's in cahoots with Slade? I mean, first there was the business with the fire last night, then there was the flashing rifle coming just before Slade attacked us. . . ."

"I don't know," Nate answered. Then he admitted, "Actually, I knew he was in prison. And as a matter of fact, he was Slade's cellmate."

"He was?" Clint punched his fist into his hand. "Then damn it, that settles it! He's got to be our man!"

"Maybe. But I saw one of Slade's men go down with a shot-out kneecap, and I'm pretty sure it was Dingo who got him."

"Well, what if Dingo shot him on purpose? You know, to make it look like he's on the level. He didn't kill the man, after all." Scratching his head, ruffling his gray hair, the lawman added, "By the way, how'd you know he and Slade shared the same cell?"

"He told me," Nate replied. "And that's another reason I don't think he's guilty. If he were in on this, why would he tell me Slade was his cellmate?"

"I don't know. Maybe it's because you're a fellow convict," Clint reasoned. "Maybe he just trusts you not to tell."

"Perhaps," the young prisoner acknowledged with a frown.

Clint started to speak but then hesitated. Finally he asked, "Nate . . . if he said he'd cut you in on part of the money if you'd keep quiet, you'd let me know, wouldn't you?"

Scowling, Nate threw the rock hard against a tree. Turning to the lawman, he then responded, "Clint, come on, I thought you knew me better than to ask a question like that. Are you still not completely convinced that my brother and I were innocent?"

"Oh, I believe you were innocent all right, but you've been serving time for it anyway—and I think it's human nature to want to get even. You may figure you're owed some of the money that's on this stage."

"If you really believe that, why are you letting me carry a gun?"

"Because I *don't* really believe it, I guess," Clint admitted with a sigh. "Hell, I'm not supposed to be on this stage anyway. If my horse hadn't gone lame, I'd already be back in Buffalo, wondering what was taking the stage so long to get there."

Nate smiled. "Well then, aren't you glad you're here with us so you can have your curiosity satisfied?"

Laughing, the lawman replied, "You know, they say curiosity once killed a cat. I just hope that doesn't hold true for sheriffs."

Suddenly Luke Hightower's voice rode the air. "Clint! Nate! The horses have got their breath back. I think we can leave, if you two are of a mind!"

"Be right there, Luke," Clint shouted back, and he and Nate turned and started toward the coach. Looking at his prisoner, the sheriff had a wry grin on his face as he remarked, "You know, I sort of hope Slade does try again. If he does, we'll burn him good." He then chuckled, adding, "Only I want you to promise to leave the fella in the top hat to me. I've never shot anyone as elegantly dressed as that."

Nate laughed, promising, "He's all yours."

They reached the coach, and everyone reboarded,

with Clint Townsend and Nate Yeager once again riding on top, their weapons held at the ready. But the vehicle had gotten no farther than a half mile when the left rear wheel suddenly seized up.

"Whoa!" Luke called to his team, hauling back on the reins again.

"What now?" Clint asked.

"If it's not one thing, it's another," Luke muttered, tying off the reins. "Somethin's wrong with one of the wheels. One of the ones in the rear, I think. Feels like it's locked up tighter than a drum."

Luke climbed down from the coach, while everyone watched with concern. Checking the wheels, he found the troublesome one and put his hand on the hub. Luke then removed some of the axle grease and rubbed it between his fingers.

"I'll be damned," he breathed.

"What is it?" Clint asked from up top.

Holding his grease-stained fingers out toward the lawman, Luke answered, "This is full of grit. Someone's put dirt in the hub." Narrowing his eyes, he observed unnecessarily, "One of us on this here stage don't want us to get through."

"But . . . who would do such a thing?" Shannon McBride, her head sticking out the window, asked in a disbelieving voice.

"I'll tell you who it is!" Sidney Durant said, climbing out of the stage and brushing himself off. "It's him!" He pointed an accusing finger up at Nate. "I warned all of you! I told you not to let an outlaw ride with us! Now look what he has done!"

"Durant, we don't know that he did it," Clint insisted.

"Well, I know he did it, whether any of the rest of you want to admit it or not!" the clerk declared, his voice self-righteous.

"Right now it don't make no difference who done it," Luke Hightower grumbled. "The thing we gotta do is get that wheel off and get all the dirty grease out of there. Then I can goop her down good with some clean grease, and we can reset the wheel and get going."

"How long is all that going to take?" Trey Farnsworth asked, sticking his head out the window.

"Not too long, if we'll just get on it," the driver answered.

Pointing up to a shadowed, snow-covered ledge some fifty feet up the side of the mountain that bordered the road, Trey noted, "We've run out of ice for the boy's stomach. Will I have time to climb up there and get some snow?"

Luke looked up at the snowbank and then nodded. "Sure, I reckon you'll have time to do that."

"Good." He looked across at Nell Gentry and told her, "Don't worry. We'll keep him comfortable."

"Thank you, Trey," she murmured, her gratitude obvious.

The gambler hopped off the stage, and the driver poked his head inside. "I'm gonna have to ask you folks to get out. Sorry about havin' to disturb the boy, but it can't be helped."

"Of course," Nell responded, helping Tad to his feet. The women and the boy then climbed off the stage.

Glancing around, Luke shook his head and observed, "Even with the jack, it's gonna take at least three of us to get this stage lifted. Sheriff, if you and Nate'll help Dingo get her raised up, I'll pull the wheel." He smiled ruefully. "I'm afraid this here jack don't do nothin' to make our job easier. All's it does is provide a base to rest the axle on once we get 'er raised." Turning to the bank clerk, he then suggested,

"Mr. Durant, you and the ladies can keep a sharp lookout for Zeke Slade and his bunch."

Tad shuffled over to the oppposite side of the road, where he found a place to lie down. With the boy safely out of the way, Nell, Shannon, and Durant took up their posts to act as lookouts.

The men began working. It proved to be hard, heavy labor, and they were well into it, sweating and shoving to make sure the coach was lifted and the jack put into position.

Suddenly Tad called out, "Mama! Come quick! I'm hurting real bad!"

Nell's head whipped around. She then looked back at Shannon and Durant and told them in a shaky voice, "I have to go to him."

Shannon watched her hurry off, and Durant offered, "Miss McBride, you can go help her if you want. I'll keep watch."

Clearly surprised by her fellow traveler's uncharacteristically generous offer, the young woman responded, "Oh, thank you, Mr. Durant! I appreciate it." Then she lifted her long skirt and hurried over to Nell and her son.

For the next few minutes, all were involved in what they were doing. The women tried to soothe the boy, while the four men grunted and groaned as they hurried to complete their job. Then suddenly an evil laugh rang out, and a loud, gruff voice taunted, "Well, now! Lookee here, would you?"

Everyone turned to see Zeke Slade holding a pistol pointed at them. Two other men were with Slade, one wearing a Mexican serape and the other wearing dirty formal striped trousers and a top hat. They, like their leader, had revolvers trained on the travelers.

"Slade!" Nate growled.

"That's right," the outlaw confirmed dryly. Then

his cadaverous face hardened, and he snarled, "Now, how about you fellas unhooking your holsters and letting your guns drop?" When Dingo started inching toward his shotgun, Slade aimed his pistol directly at him and warned, "Try it, Dingo, and you're a dead man. Maybe I should'a slit your throat five years ago instead of givin' you that nice souvenir you're wearin'. You sure did cause me a peck of trouble after rattin' on me."

Fingering his scar, Dingo looked at the outlaw with loathing. "You didn't have to kill that kid in the pen. All's he did was try to protect his property."

Smirking, Slade agreed, "That's true. But I wanted it, and that's all that mattered." He then glared at Dingo and said, "And all that matters now is that you obey me."

The shotgun guard said nothing more and moved back.

"Ah, that's more like it." Looking over at Nate, Slade cautioned, "And you, fella, you seem a mite slow in droppin' your gun. I'd get rid of it now, if I was you. And kick it out of reach."

With a slow sigh of frustration, Nate pulled his pistol out, using thumb and forefinger on the butt, and dropped it in the dirt and kicked it aside.

"Now you're bein' smart," Slade mocked.

"Yeah, but I guess I wasn't smart enough two years ago," Nate rejoined coldly. "I let you get the better of me then."

Slade squinted his eyes and studied his adversary for a moment. "Say, I know you, don't I?"

"In a manner of speaking," came the bitter reply. "My name's Nate Yeager. Does that mean anything to you?"

Laughing gleefully, the outlaw answered, "Well,

I'll be damned! Yeah, I know who you are now. You went to prison for that bank job up in Banner."

"I went to prison, but I didn't pull the job—as you well know."

Slade's dark piercing eyes narrowed. "I didn't know you was out."

"How could you? But I paid your camp a visit the other night."

A broad smile slowly spread over the outlaw's gaunt face, and he exclaimed, "So, that was you! I've been wonderin' who that was pokin' around out there in the dark. Tell me, Yeager, I thought you was supposed to be in prison for—what was it?—twenty years. How'd you get out of jail, anyway?

"I broke out."

"Is that a fact? Well, ain't that a hell of a thing!" He looked over at the two men with him. "Well now, boys, what do you think about that? Our friend here broke out of prison. Maybe we should take him into our gang. We need a good man now, what with these fellas killin' Murdock and bustin' up Kelly's knee so bad we had to leave him back there in the hills. What do you say, Yeager? You want to join up?"

"No, thanks," Nate answered. "I have other plans in mind. Matter of fact, I've been looking forward to meeting you for a long time."

"I'll bet you have," Slade responded with a laugh. "But right now I'm more interested in the money. Where's it at?"

"It's in the coach," Sidney Durant spoke up. "I'll get it for you."

Durant opened the door to the stagecoach and took out the satchel, and then he opened the bag and reached inside. "You'll find it all here. I've put it in packets of one thousand dollars each."

"Just throw the whole thing over here, Banker," Slade ordered.

Durant drew himself up to his full five feet three inches. "I most certainly will not!" he replied indignantly. "I will give you exactly fifty thousand dollars, which is your share. Fifty thousand and no more. And I trust you brought me a horse."

Turning to his men, Slade began mimicking Durant. "'I trust you brought me a horse.'" He laughed uproariously, and his cohorts laughed with him. Then he turned back to face Durant, and the smile left his face. "There's somethin' you don't understand, Banker. It's *all* my share," he said coldly.

"Now, just you wait a minute!" Durant shouted. "Who set this up? I did! I told you about the money, I built up the fire last night to guide you to us when we left the trail, and I sabotaged the stage so it would have to—"

That was as far as Durant got, because Slade raised his revolver and shot him without so much as blinking an eye.

"What? . . . No . . . " Sidney Durant gasped, clutching his chest and looking down in surprise as blood spilled through his fingers. "You cheated me . . . you cheated—" He took a step toward Slade and then pitched forward and fell facedown in the dirt.

"Troublesome little son of a bitch, wasn't he?" the gang leader muttered.

"Mr. Durant!" Shannon McBride screamed as she raced to the clerk. Kneeling beside him, she put her hand on his neck.

"Ain't no need in checkin' on him, Missy. He was dead by the time he hit the ground," the outlaw remarked.

Shannon looked up at the outlaw with her eyes blazing fire. "Do you think you're going to get away with shooting him down in cold blood like that?" she asked angrily. "We all saw you do it!"

"Yeah, and I would've thought you'd be happy to see him go first," the outlaw retorted. "After all, he's the one who got you into this mess. But it don't matter none. You're all gonna have to die." He looked at her appraisingly. "Too bad about you though, honey. You sure are a looker."

"Slade, answer one question for me first, will you?" Nate Yeager suddenly asked.

"Sure, why not?"

"When you killed my brother two years ago and framed me for the bank robbery, why didn't you kill me, too?"

"What good would that have done?" Slade replied, amusement in his eyes. "If I'd killed both of you, the posse wouldn't have even slowed down. By me leavin' you alive like that, that dumb marshal figured he was on to somethin', so he forgot all about me and my boys so he could take you back for a big trial."

"Then he *was* telling the truth?" Clint Townsend asked. "He was innocent all along?"

Slade laughed. "As innocent as a newborn babe. Or"—he added with a chuckle—"you might say a lamb being led to the slaughter."

"Thank you, Slade," Nate put in. "You've just cleared me."

"Yeah? Well, it's too bad you won't be alive to enjoy it."

Nodding slowly, Nate then asked the outlaw how he had arranged the deal with Durant. He had no interest in knowing the answer, it was merely a ploy to keep the man talking, playing for time, because unseen by Slade and his men, Trey Farnsworth was slipping quietly down the side of the mountain from where he had gone for snow. Finally halting about ten feet above and behind the outlaws, Trey's right hand held the revolver he normally carried in his holster, while in his left was the derringer that he carried hidden up his sleeve.

Then he turned the pistol around so that he was holding it by the barrel. He made a tiny pitching motion with his hand, and Nate nodded almost imperceptibly that he understood.

"Turn around, Slade!" the gambler suddenly shouted. At the same time, Trey tossed the revolver through the air toward Nate.

Startled by the unexpected voice, Slade and his men turned abruptly, their weapons aimed high. Trey fired his derringer, then dived behind a rock. Although he was out of range for such a weapon, it was not important that he hit anything, just that he provide a diversion.

Zeke Slade, Jim Silverthorn, and Slim Hawkins all immediately fired back at the gambler, despite the fact that he was well protected.

"Slade!" Nate shouted.

Slade spun back around and it was evident that he was shocked to see the revolver in Nate's hand. The two men fired simultaneously, but while Slade's bullet slammed harmlessly into the side of the coach, Nate's slug found its mark. The outlaw leader clutched his throat, and blood spurted between his fingers. A startled look on his face, he stared wordlessly at his enemy and then sank to his knees. He coughed once and then crumpled to the ground, his eyes staring vacantly.

In the meantime, Clint, Luke, and Dingo managed to recover their own weapons, and a gun battle erupted. With the opening shots, Nell and Shannon threw themselves on the ground, covering Tad's body with their own. The little valley echoed with the sounds of gunfire, and bullets whistled off the rocks.

With no time for anyone to leap for cover, the men shot it out at near point-blank range. The two remaining outlaws were badly outnumbered. Disorganized, they shot wildly, barely coming close to their foes. Nate fired at the outlaw wearing the serape, leaving the one in the top hat—as promised—to Clint Townsend. He thought he had the man pinned down when suddenly a bullet whistled close to his ear. Swearing loudly, Nate aimed carefully and fired, and Slim Hawkins screamed in pain and then fell flat.

Clint then took out his quarry. After blowing a hole in Jim Silverthorn's top hat, whisking it off the man's head, the sheriff planted another slug right between the outlaw's eyes. Silverthorn's fingers froze around the handle of his revolver as he sank to his knees and then flopped onto his back, staring sightlessly at the sky.

For a long moment, everyone stood rooted to the spot, as if in shock. The air hung heavy with the smell of spent gunpowder, and a billowing cloud of blue smoke drifted lazily away.

"Is everyone all right down there?" Trey Farnsworth called, rising cautiously from behind the rock.

"Gambling Man," Clint Townsend shouted, holding onto his arm, which had sustained a flesh wound, "you got my word: You can stay in Buffalo as long as you want. No matter what kind of committee the folks may get up against you, I'll insist you always be welcome."

"If they go against him, they're going to have to go against me, too," Nell Gentry added, smiling broadly.

"And I'll be standing right beside you, Nell," Shannon McBride agreed.

Climbing down from the hillside, Trey suggested, "How about if we all save the praise for when we get back to Buffalo? And the sooner we get that wheel back on, the sooner we'll be there. Don't forget, we've got a sick boy on our hands."

Nodding, Luke Hightower said, "Right you are Okay, men. Let's get to it."

As Nate stepped to the coach, he looked at Clint and asked, "What about that guy with the bullet through his knee? He's somewhere back on the trail."

Nodding, the lawman responded, "The way he was losing blood, he won't get far. As soon as we reach Buffalo, I'll send out a couple of men to go after him."

As soon as the wheel had been remounted, every one reboarded the stagecoach. With the threat of robbery no longer hanging over their heads, Nate Yeager and Clint Townsend were once again able to ride inside.

Just as Clint was about to step aboard, he looked up at Dingo and said, "By the way. There's something I've been meaning to ask you. I saw you go into the telegraph office in Medicine Bow just before we departed, and I gotta confess that for a while there, I thought maybe you'd sent some kind of message to Slade. Now, I know it's none of my business to ask—"

"That's all right, Sheriff," Dingo cut in. "I ain't got nothin' to hide. Fact is, Luke sent me over to get a message off to Miss McBride's papa. He promised he'd let Mr. McBride know that his daughter'd got in okay on the train and was headin' to home."

Smiling sheepishly, the lawman said, "I guess I could've saved myself a whole lot of wondering if I'd just asked you before."

Dingo grinned, and for a moment he looked closer to thirty-five than fifty. "Yeah," he agreed. "I guess you could have."

Chapter Ten

It was evident that Tad Gentry's condition was worsening. His pain had increased, his fever was up, and his pulse rate was fast. Trey Farnsworth never left the boy's side, keeping a steady watch over him.

He looked up at Nell, whose face was pale with fear, and his heart went out to the beautiful redhead. Putting his hand over hers, he said softly, "He'll make it. I promise."

A tear trickled down Nell's cheek, and her lower lip trembled. "How can you be so sure?" she asked, her voice barely a whisper.

"I just am. Trust me."

She gave the gambler a small smile. "I do, you know. I really do."

He smiled back reassuringly and then once again put all his attention on the gravely ill child.

Whenever the road would allow it, Luke Hightower kept the horses going at a fast trot. They were coming down from the mountain now, and the road was a great deal better than it had been. As a result, they were able to make much better time than had been possible since leaving the main road.

Finally they rolled into Buffalo at twenty minutes before midnight, and Luke did not even bother to stop at the stage depot. Instead he urged the team into a gallop, and the coach rumbled down the main street until it reached Dr. Robert Presnell's office.

The coach lurched to a halt, and Trey leapt down and ran to the physician's door. He pounded hard for a few moments and then lights came on inside. Several more moments passed, and then the door was flung open. An elderly man clad in a nightshirt stood in the doorway holding a kerosene lamp.

"Yes? What can I do for you?"

"I'm looking for Dr. Presnell."

"I am Dr. Presnell," the kindly looking white-haired man said, stepping out onto the porch.

"Thank God!" Trey breathed. "We have a critically ill child on board, Doctor. Have you a stretcher?"

"'Course I have a stretcher," the doctor replied, obviously surprised by the question. "This is a medical facility, you know."

Nodding, the gambler said, "I'm sorry. I didn't mean to imply. . . " His words trailed off, and he turned and hurried back to the stage.

"Come on, Dingo," Nate Yeager said. "Help me get the stretcher." Then he and the shotgun guard hurried into the doctor's office. A few minutes later they returned, carrying the stretcher between them.

Working carefully from inside, Trey and Clint Townsend lifted the boy from where he had been lying between his mother and Shannon McBride and gently carried him to the doorway. Luke Hightower guided Tad onto the stretcher, and then Dingo and Nate carried the boy into the doctor's office and placed him on the examining table.

Everyone else had by then crowded inside.

"Doctor, the boy has appendicitis," Trey explained.

The physician smiled patronizingly at the man in black. "Why don't you just let me be the judge of that?" he replied. Looking Trey up and down, he added, "I'd say medical diagnoses are a bit out of your field, sir." As he started to examine Tad, he asked, "But just out of curiosity, what makes you think the child is suffering from appendicitis?"

"He has severe abdominal pain that started near the umbilicus, then localized in the lower right side. He has no appetite and has suffered from nausea and fever. His pulse has remained strong but is rapid."

The amused expression left Presnell's face and he looked at Trey in surprise. "You're right," he said. "Those *are* the symptoms of appendicitis."

"I stabilized the condition by the application of ice packs. It numbed him against the pain and kept the appendix from rupturing so far, but you're going to have to operate, Doctor. His appendix must come out."

"Let's not be so hasty."

"No, that's just it, Dr. Presnell. We *must* be hasty. This child has been suffering for days. We've waited as long as we can."

"Mister, I'm not sure you understand what you're saying," the physician rejoined. "You're talking about abdominal invasive surgery." Presnell shook his head. "I can't do that. Why, it could kill the boy."

"There is some degree of danger, of course, but it can be greatly minimized if you do the procedure properly," Trey insisted.

"And I suppose you are going to tell me how to do it properly?"

"If you wish," the gambler answered, ignoring the mocking tone. "Make a transverse incision, then ligate the meso-appendix and remove it by the Paquelin cautery. Tie off the stump and cauterize it, then close him back up. But make certain that your hands and the

instruments you use are absolutely clean. You mus
introduce nothing into the wound that could caus
infection."

Nell Gentry stood with her mouth open. Finall
she asked, "Trey, who *are* you? You are obviously no
just a gambler."

"I am now," he told her.

"And before now?"

Trey let out a long sigh. "I was a doctor," h
admitted.

"What is your name?" Presnell asked.

"Farnsworth."

"Farnsworth . . . Farnsworth. . . . See here, yo
wouldn't be Preston Farnsworth, would you?"

"Yes. Preston Gordon Farnsworth. The Third. That'
where Trey comes from," he added to Nell.

"Well, I'll be damned," Presnell said. "Doctor, th
whole world is wondering what happened to you."

Looking more confused than ever, Nell remarked
"Dr. Presnell, you've obviously heard of Trey."

"My dear, your friend here was one of the bes
surgeons in the country. Why, I read about him ever
out here." Turning to the gambler, he asked, "But wha
happened to you, Dr. Farnsworth? You just droppec
out of sight, as I recall."

"Look," Trey said. "We can discuss all this later
The most important thing now is to operate on the boy
If you don't get that appendix out soon, it's going t
rupture. And if it ruptures, I don't have to tell you tha
the boy will probably die."

Shaking his head firmly, Presnell declared, "It'
not that simple."

"If you wish, I will assist," Trey offered.

Presnell shook his head again. "You don't under
stand. I simply can't do it. I don't have the skills fo
such an operation. And even if I did, my hands jus

wouldn't cooperate." He held up his fingers, and Trey saw that they had been twisted and gnarled by arthritis.

"But you must have performed operations," Trey insisted.

"Oh, yes. I've set a few bones and extracted more than my share of bullets. I'm all right as a country doctor, handing out medicine and the like, but I can't handle a scalpel. No, Doctor, if this boy's appendix is going to come out, then *you* are the one who will have to take it out."

The gambler's face turned pale. "Me? No, absolutely not. The boy is your patient, not mine."

"Oh, Trey, you can do the operation, can't you?" Nell asked, wringing her hands and looking up at him pleadingly.

"Nell, you don't know what you're asking of me," Trey said.

"Oh, but I do know," Nell replied. "I'm asking you to save my son."

Trey started to object, but he quickly realized that there was no other option if the boy was to survive. His decision was forced when Tad clutched his side and cried out in agony. Bending over the boy, the gambler examined him and realized that the appendix was on the verge of rupturing.

He stood up, his face tortured. "Dammit!" he whispered. Closing his eyes, he pinched the bridge of his nose for a moment and then took a deep breath and let out a long and slow sigh. "All right," he finally relented. "All right, I'll do the operation."

"I'll assist," Presnell offered. "What instruments will you need?"

Trey told him and then asked, "Do you have any carbolic acid?"

"Yes, I do," the elderly physician replied.

"Would you please pour it into a tray and then empty my instruments into that tray?"

"Yes, of course, Doctor," Presnell replied.

Trey then started preparing Tad for the operation, washing him thoroughly and then administering chloroform to anesthetize him. He then scrubbed his own hands repeatedly and, with that done, returned to his patient.

Finally looking up from the youngster, Trey faced Nell Gentry and suggested, "It would be best if you wait outside. Operations are very bloody, and I don't want you to worry at the sight of so much blood coming from your son."

Nell was clearly reluctant to leave her son, but she went into the anteroom, joining the others, who were all waiting anxiously.

Looking over his shoulder at the white-haired physician, Trey told him, "Doctor, I'm going to ask that you wash your hands as thoroughly as I just did."

While Presnell was following instructions, Trey stood over the boy. His heart was beating fast as he held his hands out in front of him, palms up. Though he had done many appendectomies in his career, always considering them simple operations, it had been a long time since he had last performed one. His confidence had been shattered by his fiancée's death, and now this boy and his mother were much more than an impersonal patient and family. They had become very important to him—just as Deborah had been important to him when he had operated on her tumor against the advice of his fellow surgeons.

He breathed a quick prayer; then, when Presnell joined him at the table and handed him the scalpel, Trey took it in hand and began.

Cutting into the abdomen, he bared the swollen appendix. He worked quickly and efficiently and began

aking the incisions and slicing through the tissue
quired to remove the diseased organ.

Suddenly the boy went into respiratory arrest.
rey felt his own heart begin pounding, and he cried,
No! Not again! I won't let this happen again!"

Working desperately, he pulled Tad out of the crisis
ad reestablished a steady heartbeat and respiration.
Ie was sweating profusely, and Dr. Presnell dabbed
auze on the surgeon's forehead, mopping it dry.

"That was close, son," Presnell breathed.

"Too close," Trey agreed.

The older man smiled. "But close doesn't count,
fter all."

Nodding, Trey admitted, "No, I suppose it doesn't,
oes it?"

Minutes after that, he removed the diseased organ
ad began closing up the wound. With the last suture
nally in place, he sighed with relief and then put the
loodied scalpel back into the tray and walked wearily
the door of the surgery.

He leaned against the doorjamb for a moment,
tting his heart slow down, and then pulled open the
oor.

Nell, who had been pacing anxiously, stopped short
ad then rushed to him. "How—?"

"He's going to be just fine," he cut in. "Tad's a
trong little boy, and he's well on his way to recovery.
here's nothing to worry about now."

With a shout of joy, Nell threw herself into Trey's
rms.

A week later, Tad was released from the doctor's
linic, and Nell celebrated with a dinner in her newly
eopened hotel. She invited everyone who had been on
he stage, plus Dr. Presnell and Shannon's father, Kevin,
ad Luke Hightower's wife and son, Billy.

It was an exceptionally happy dinner. Tad wa
healthy again, as evidenced by the return of an appetit
that let him eat two pieces of apple pie. Shanno
McBride's father, Kevin, was delighted to have hi
daughter home again. And Nate Yeager was celebratin
the fact that he had just received official notificatio
that the original court order that had sent him to priso
had been reversed. Further, he had received a fu
pardon from the territorial governor for the priso
break and stealing the visiting lawyer's horse, clothe
and gun.

"I suppose you'll be staying on out at your ranch,
Kevin McBride remarked to Nate. "You'll be wanting t
build it up again."

"I'd like to, yes, sir," Nate responded. "Of course
it's going to take me a while to get back to the poir
Cole and I had reached before he was killed and I wa
sent to prison, but I intend to do just that."

"Perhaps it won't take you as long as you think,
Kevin suggested.

"Why? What do you mean?"

He smiled broadly. "Well, let's just say I lik
having good neighbors. What if I loaned you a hundre
head of cattle, bulls, and cows, to get you started
Would you accept it?"

"Well, sure!" Nate exclaimed, a grin lighting up hi
handsome face. "That would be wonderful! I mean
that's much more than just being neighborly! Actually,
don't know how I could ever thank you, Mr. McBride.

Kevin chuckled. "Young man, consider it the act o
a selfish parent. I don't want my daughter going back t
Boston, and I figure having you around here might jus
keep her in Wyoming." He laughed, adding, "I have
feeling from the way you two look at each other that it
all going to be in the family anyway."

Nate's grin got even wider, and he reached ove

and took Shannon's hand. "Mr. McBride, if I have anything to say about it, that's exactly the way it's going to be."

"Well," Dr. Presnell spoke up, "now that that's settled, I wonder if we could prevail upon Dr. Farnsworth to stay here as well. I could use a young partner—and Wyoming could certainly use a good surgeon." He smiled at the younger physician and asked, "What do you say, Trey?"

"I don't know," Trey replied. He turned to Nell, gazed at her lovingly, and then asked, "What do you think? Does Wyoming need me?"

"I don't know about Wyoming," Nell answered, putting her hand over his, her brown eyes sparkling with pleasure. "But I sure do."

STAGECOACH STATION 49:
GILA BEND
By Hank Mitchum

When the travelers on the stagecoach from Yuma to Tucson begin their journey, only one of them realizes that his fate will be decided in the town of Gila Bend. That man, Rado Kane, is a professional gunfighter who has been hired to take on a vicious assassin there. Although Kane is swift and accurate, his ethics dictate that he avoid killing whenever possible—and it looks as if that code is about to be put to the test.

Also aboard is Crystal Richmond, a dancer whose dreams of success were dashed in San Francisco. Heading to Tucson to change her luck, the beautiful young brunette is attracted to Kane and tries to get him to give up the life of a gunhawk, all the while fighting off the attentions of Gideon Cull, a traveling preacher. Unknown to Crystal, Cull has often provided spiritual comfort to grieving widows—only to ease them prematurely into the afterlife, pocketing the material goods they leave behind.

The passengers don't realize that the coach is being trailed by two parties: Cull's former accomplice, who has come to collect his share of the ill-gotten goods, and a wily Mexican bandit and his gang, seeking quick riches. But as their paths converge, violence is about to erupt, threatening to alter the futures of all involved—for better or worse—as they near the little town of Gila Bend.

Read GILA BEND, *on sale September 1990 wherever Bantam paperbacks are sold.*

★ WAGONS WEST ★

This continuing, magnificent saga recounts the adventures of a brave band of settlers, all of different backgrounds, all sharing one dream— to find a new and better life.

☐ 26822	**INDEPENDENCE! #1**	$4.50
☐ 26162	**NEBRASKA! #2**	$4.50
☐ 26242	**WYOMING! #3**	$4.50
☐ 26072	**OREGON! #4**	$4.50
☐ 26070	**TEXAS! #5**	$4.50
☐ 26377	**CALIFORNIA! #6**	$4.50
☐ 26546	**COLORADO! #7**	$4.50
☐ 26069	**NEVADA! #8**	$4.50
☐ 26163	**WASHINGTON! #9**	$4.50
☐ 26073	**MONTANA! #10**	$4.50
☐ 26184	**DAKOTA! #11**	$4.50
☐ 26521	**UTAH! #12**	$4.50
☐ 26071	**IDAHO! #13**	$4.50
☐ 26367	**MISSOURI! #14**	$4.50
☐ 27141	**MISSISSIPPI! #15**	$4.50
☐ 25247	**LOUISIANA! #16**	$4.50
☐ 25622	**TENNESSEE! #17**	$4.50
☐ 26022	**ILLINOIS! #18**	$4.50
☐ 26533	**WISCONSIN! #19**	$4.50
☐ 26849	**KENTUCKY! #20**	$4.50
☐ 27065	**ARIZONA! #21**	$4.50
☐ 27458	**NEW MEXICO! #22**	$4.50
☐ 27703	**OKLAHOMA! #23**	$4.50
☐ 28180	**CELEBRATION! #24**	$4.50